laid waste

JULIA GFRÖRER

FANTAGRAPHICS BOOKS, INC.

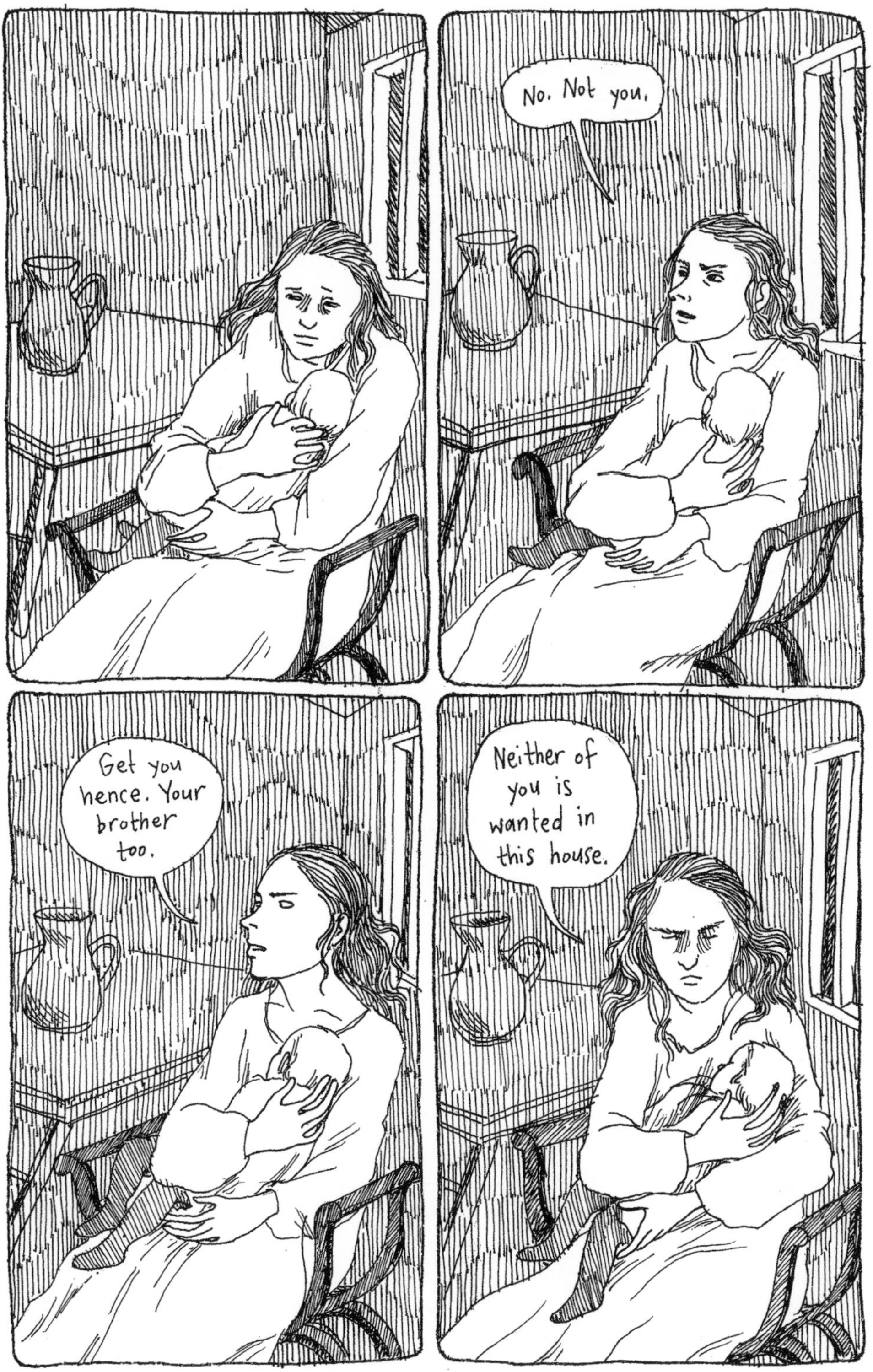
No. Not you.
Get you hence. Your brother too.
Neither of you is wanted in this house.

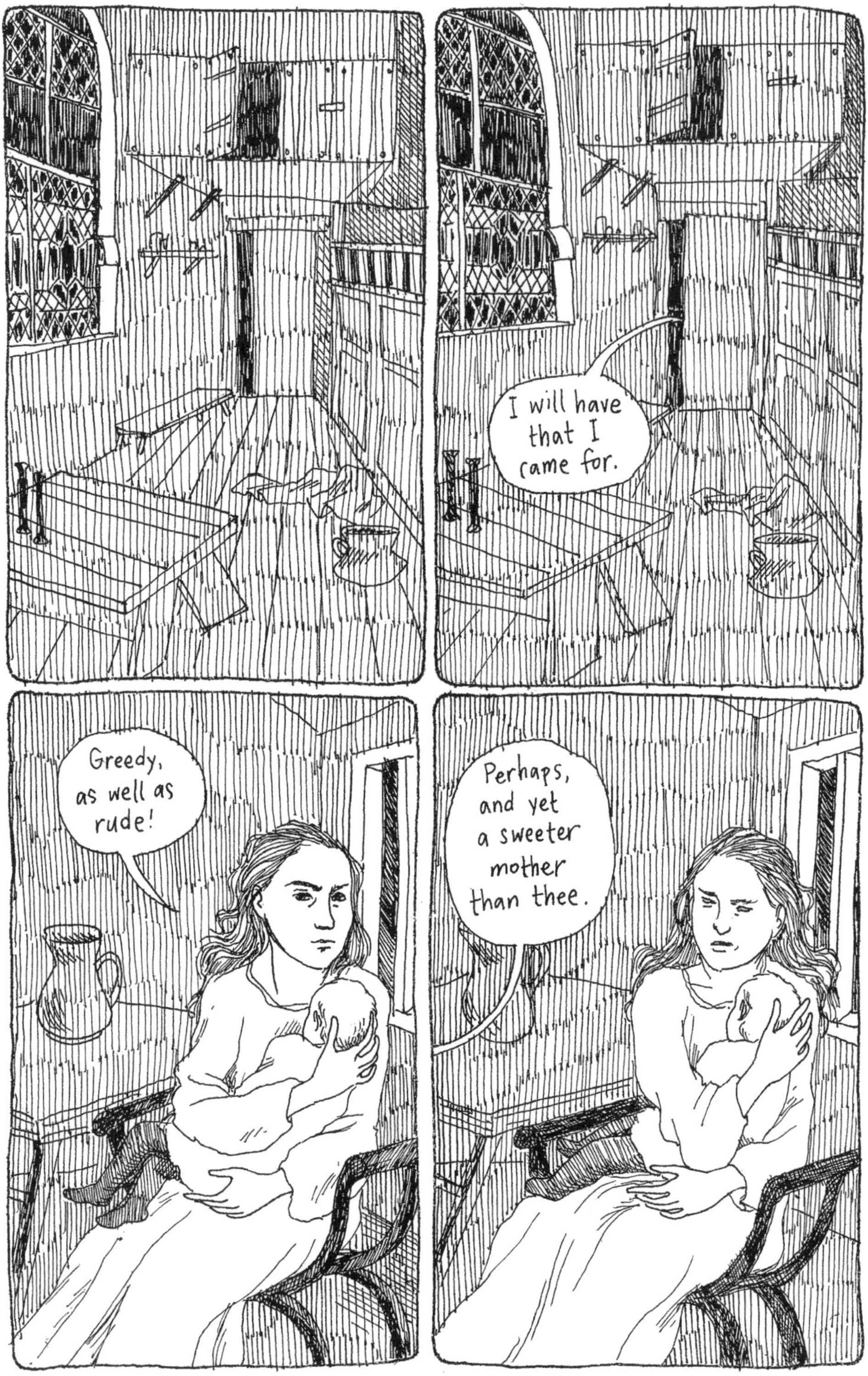
I will have that I came for.
Greedy, as well as rude!
Perhaps, and yet a sweeter mother than thee.

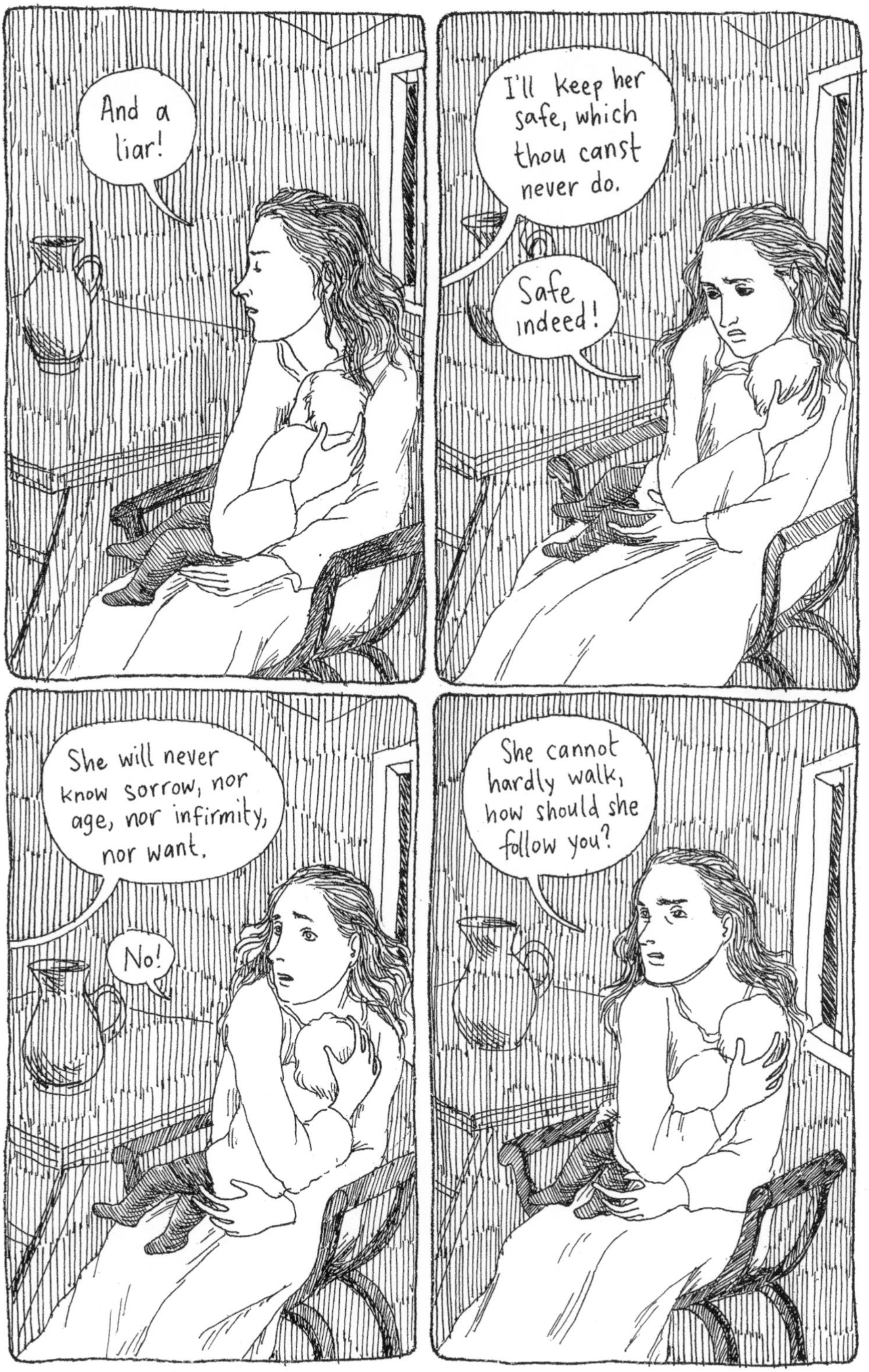
And a liar!
I'll keep her safe, which thou canst never do.
Safe indeed!
She will never know sorrow, nor age, nor infirmity, nor want.
No!
She cannot hardly walk, how should she follow you?

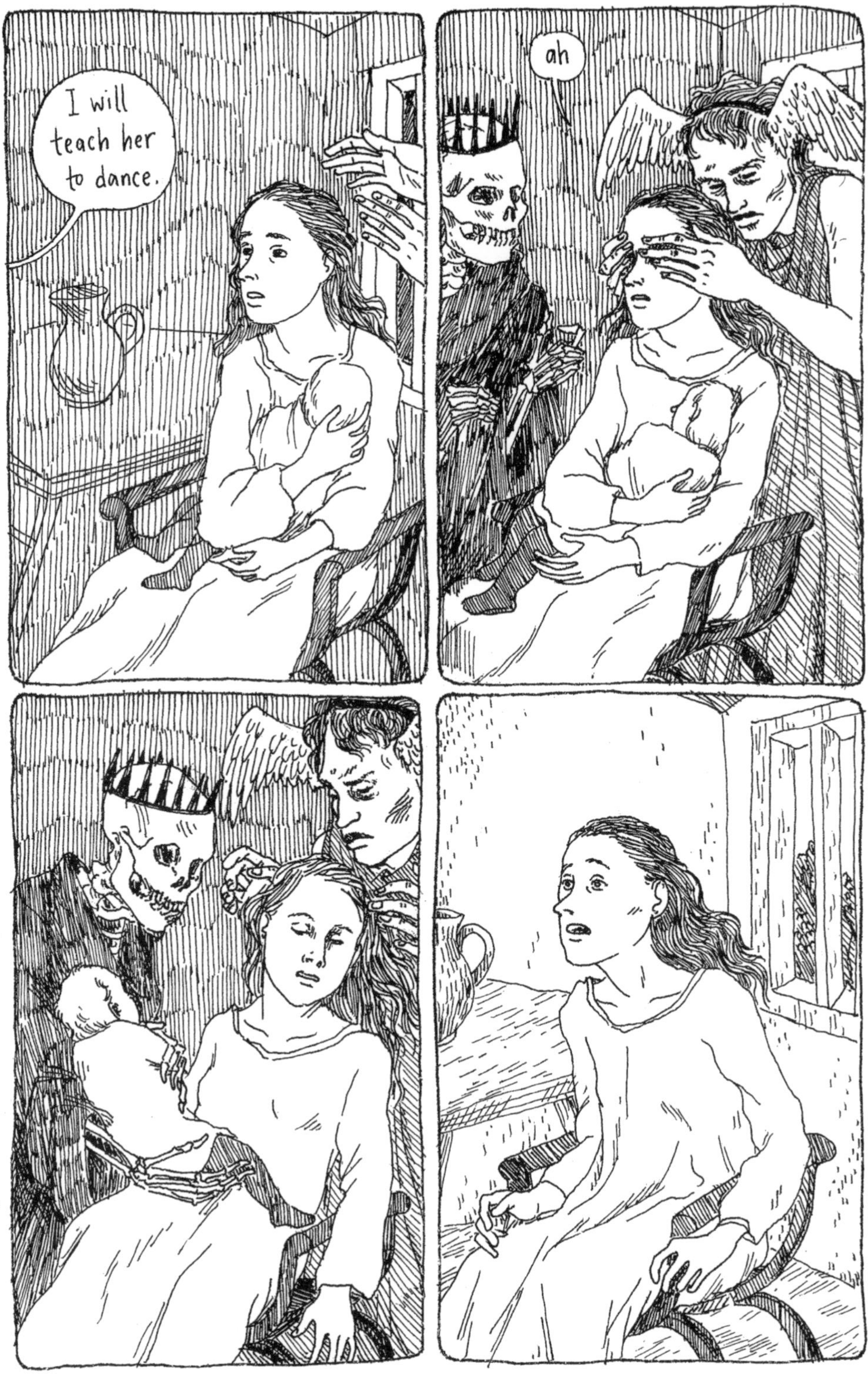
I will teach her to dance.
ah

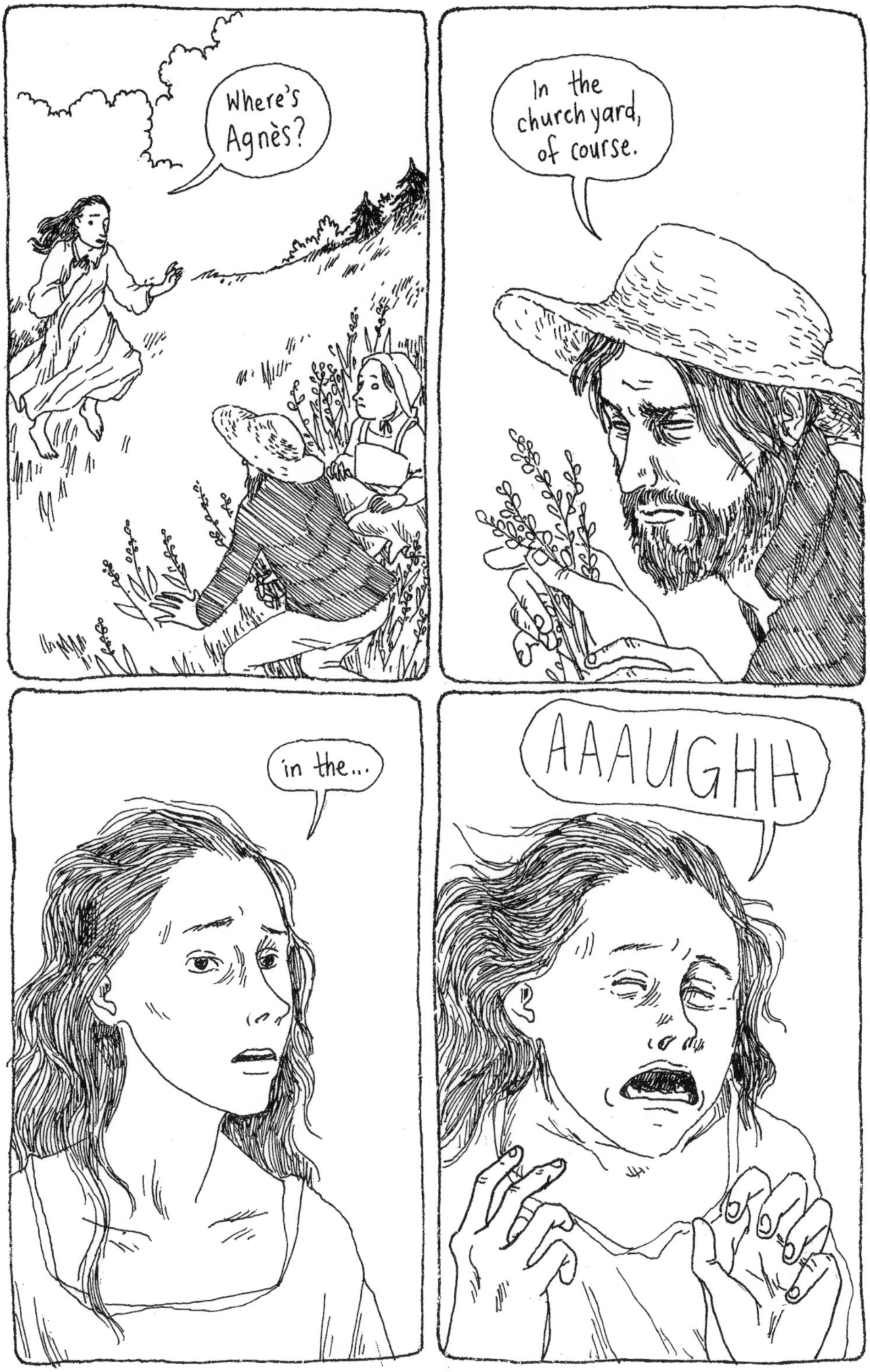
Where's Agnès?
In the churchyard, of course.
in the...
AAAUGHH

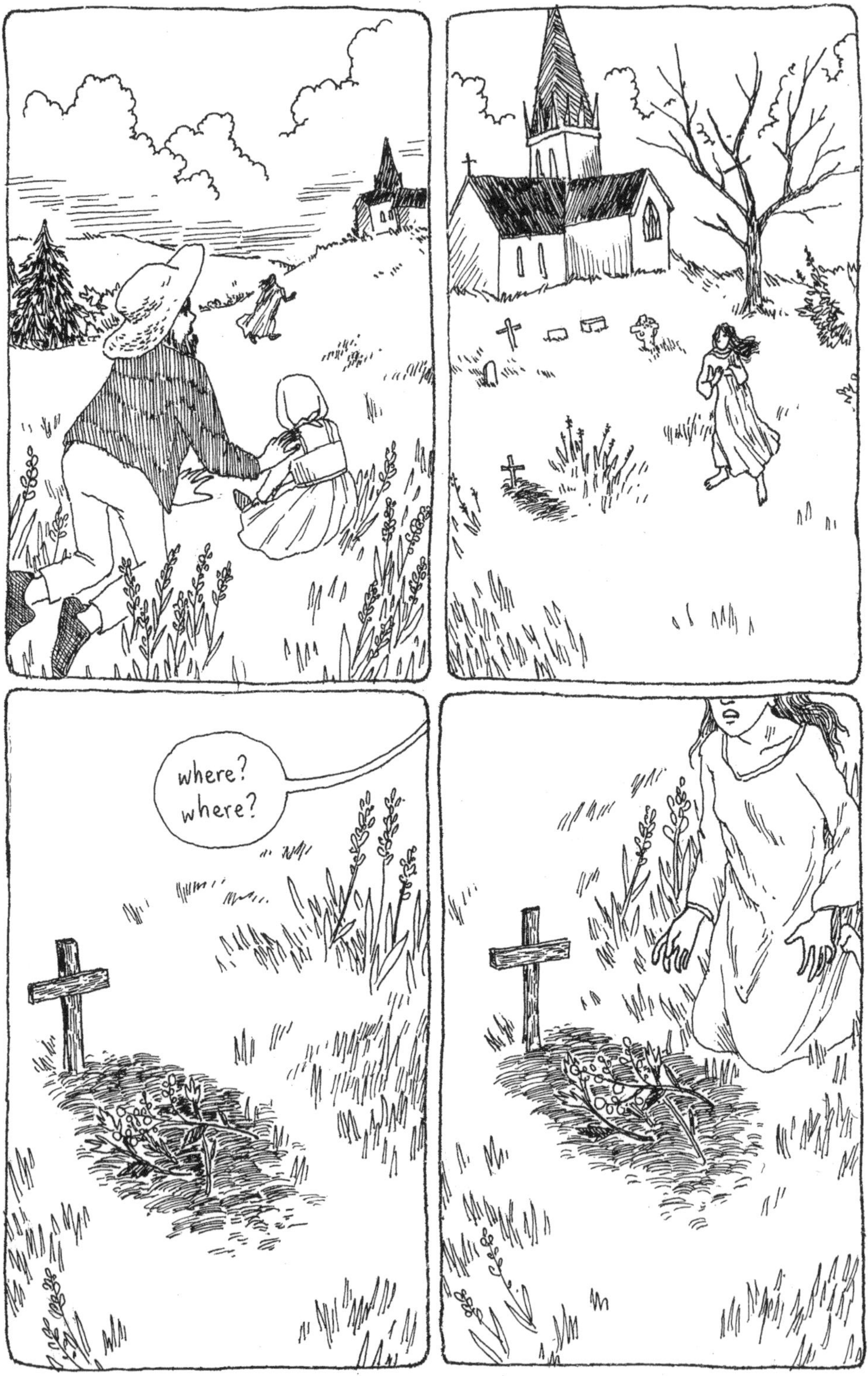
where? where?

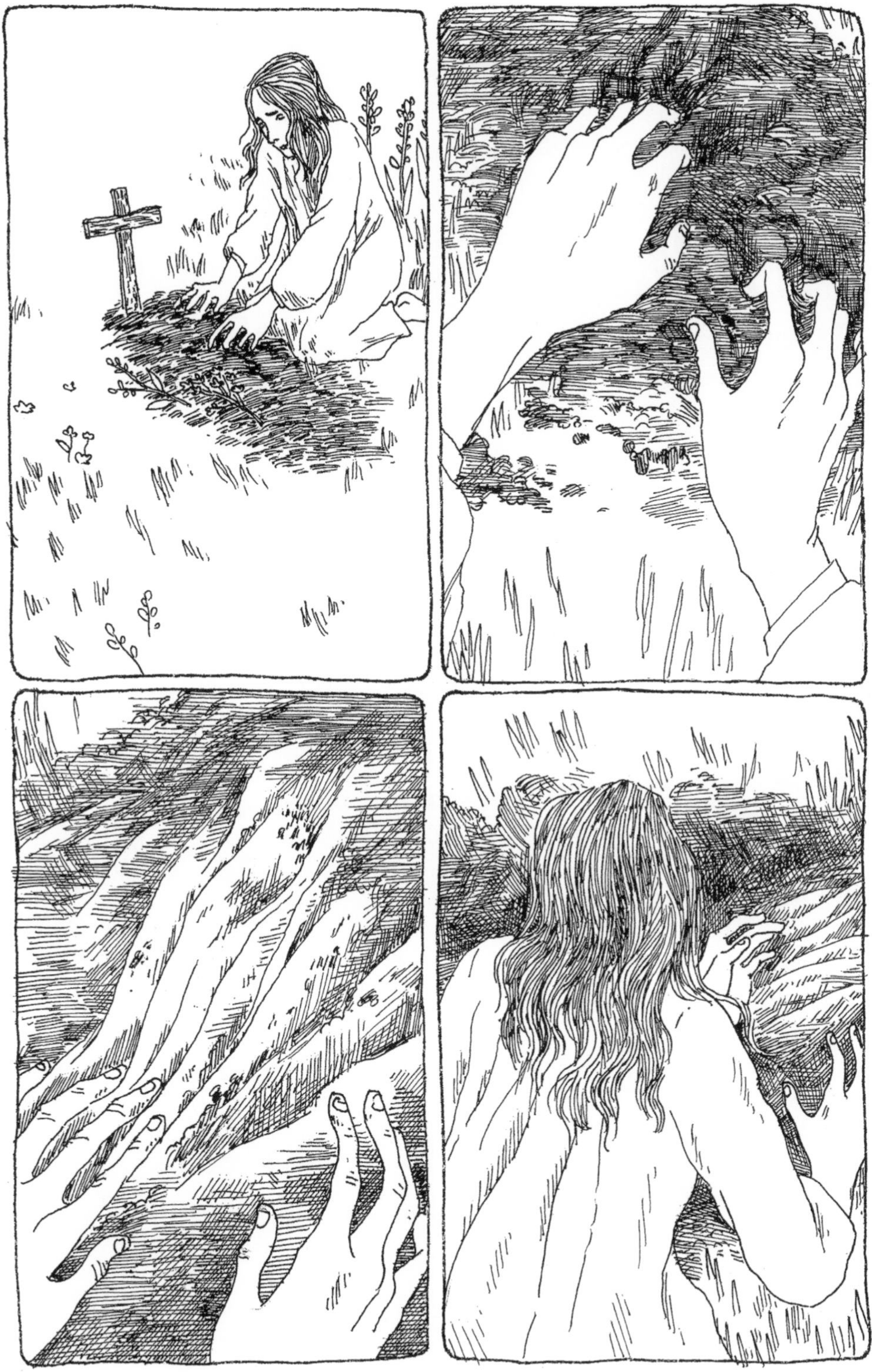

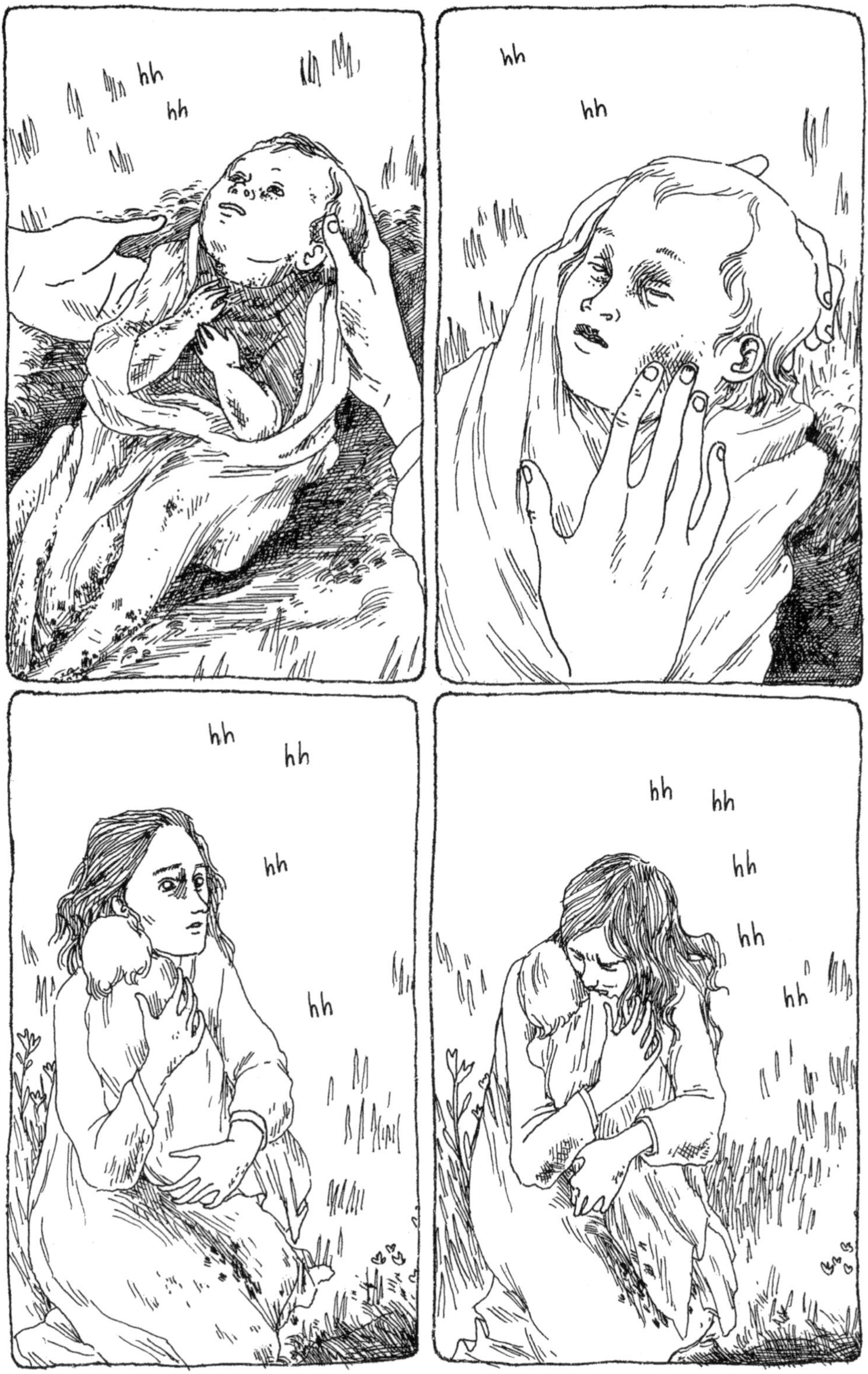
hh
hh
hh
hh
hh
hh
hh
hh
hh
hh
hh
hh
hh
hh

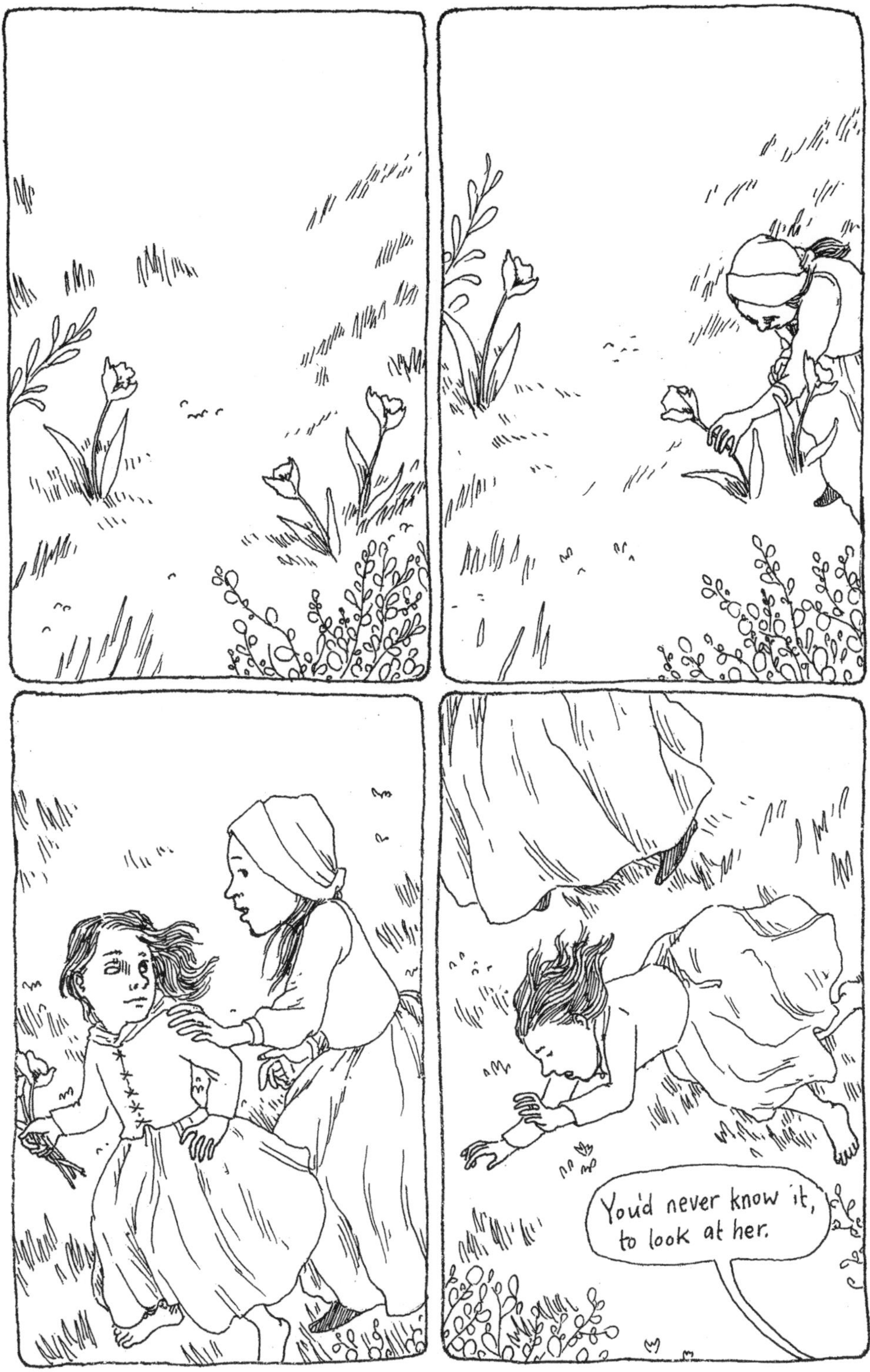
You'd never know it, to look at her.

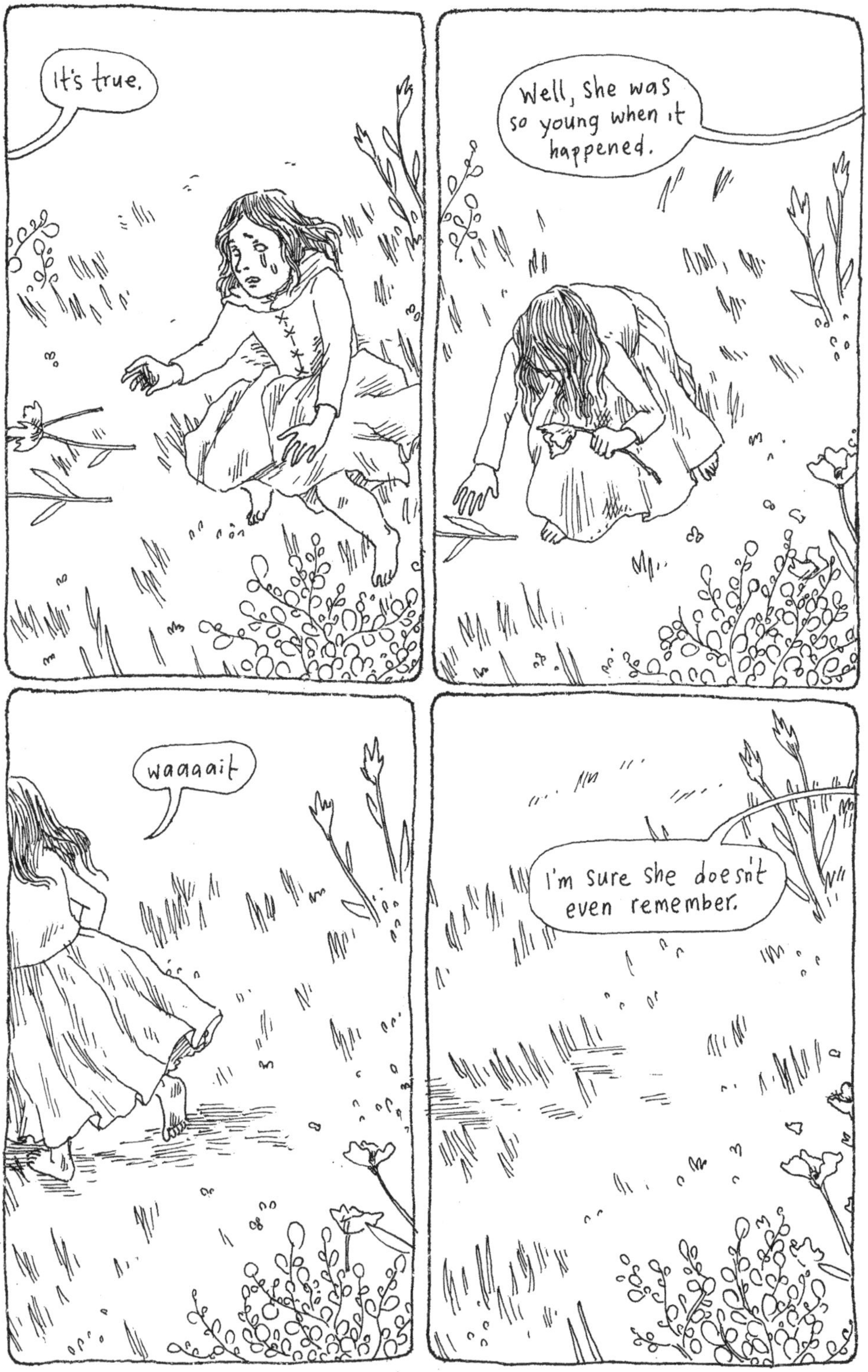
It's true.
Well, she was so young when it happened.
waaaait
I'm sure she doesn't even remember.

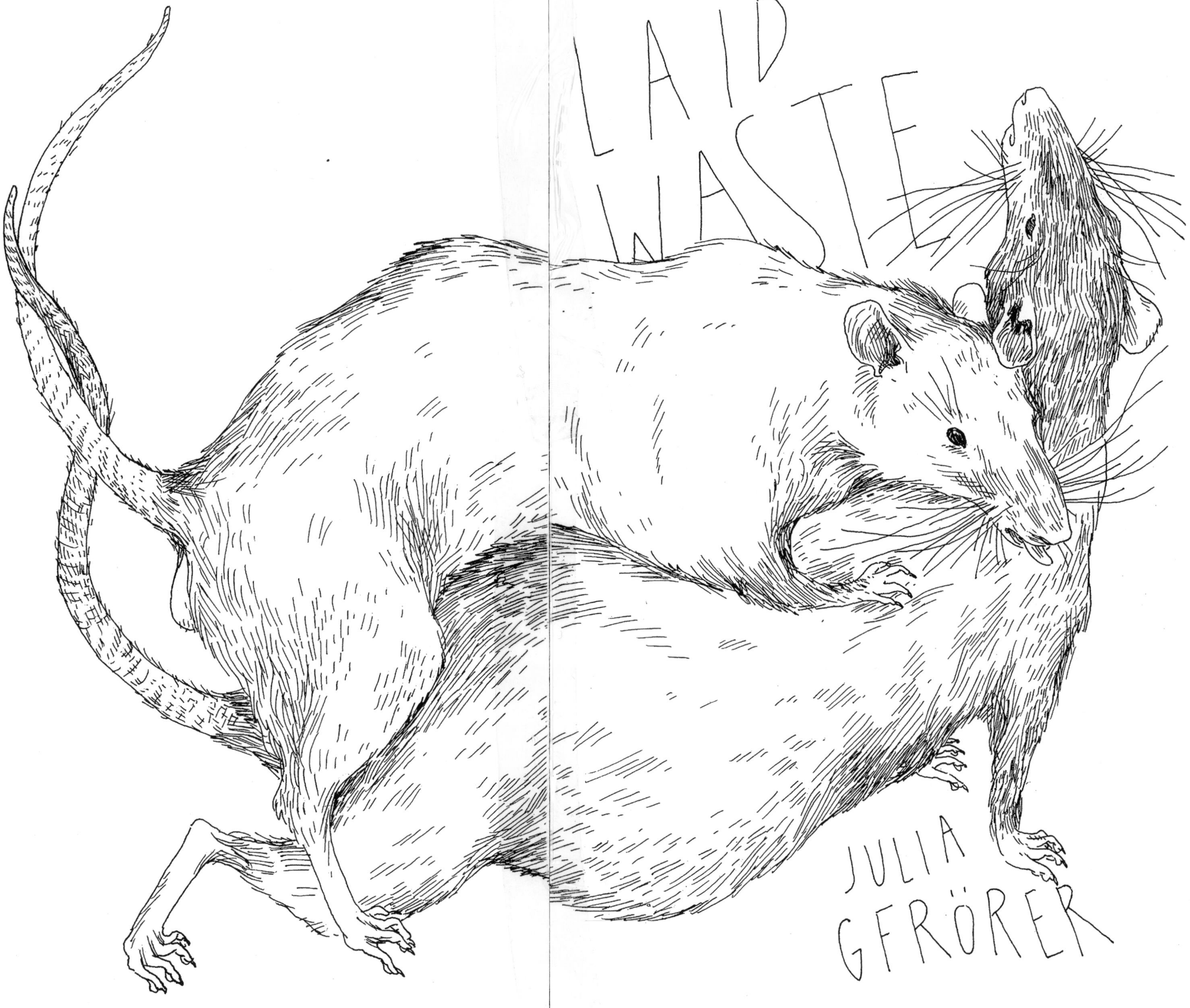
LAID
WASTE
JULIA
GFRÖRER

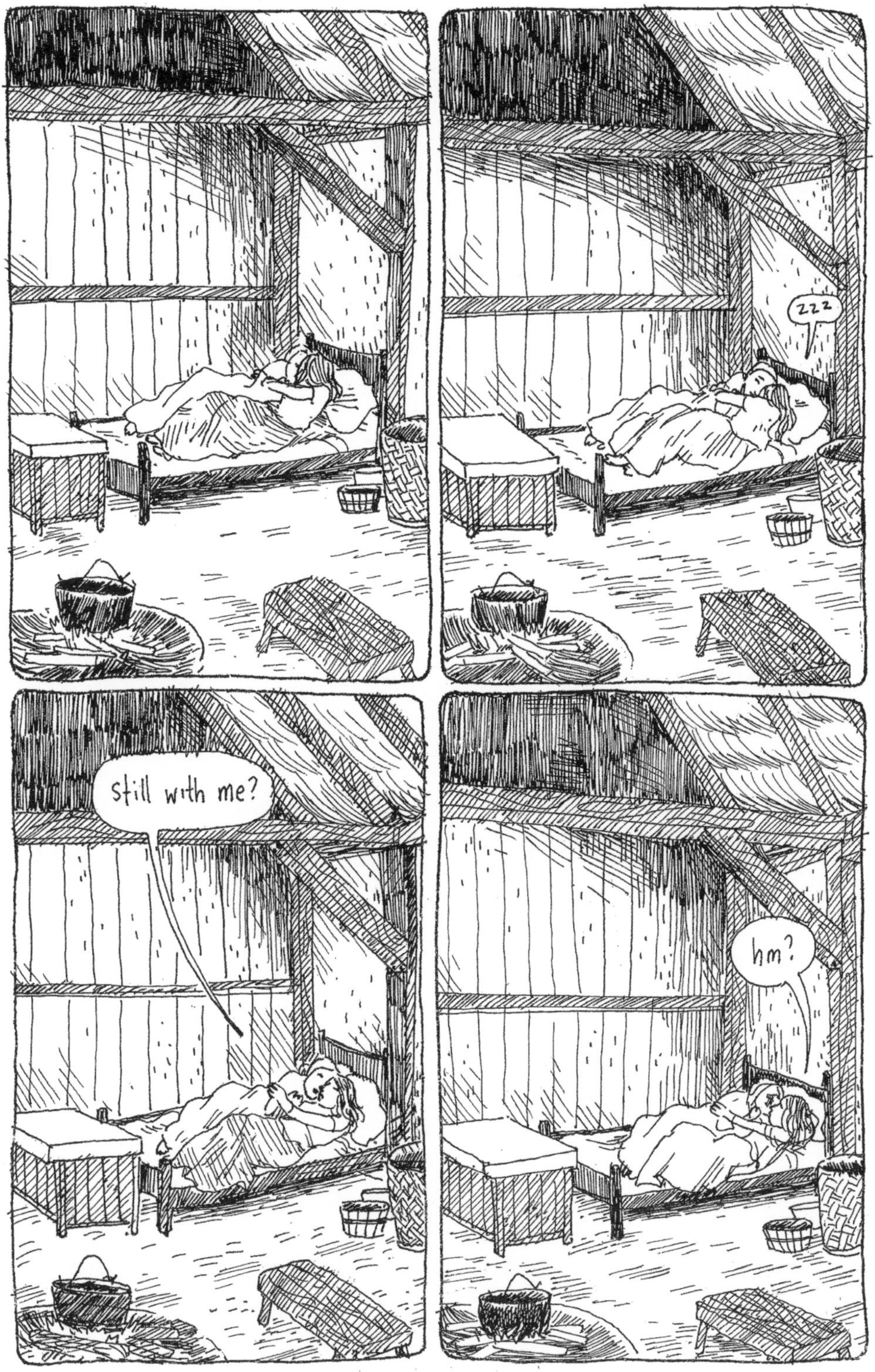
zzz
still with me?
hm?

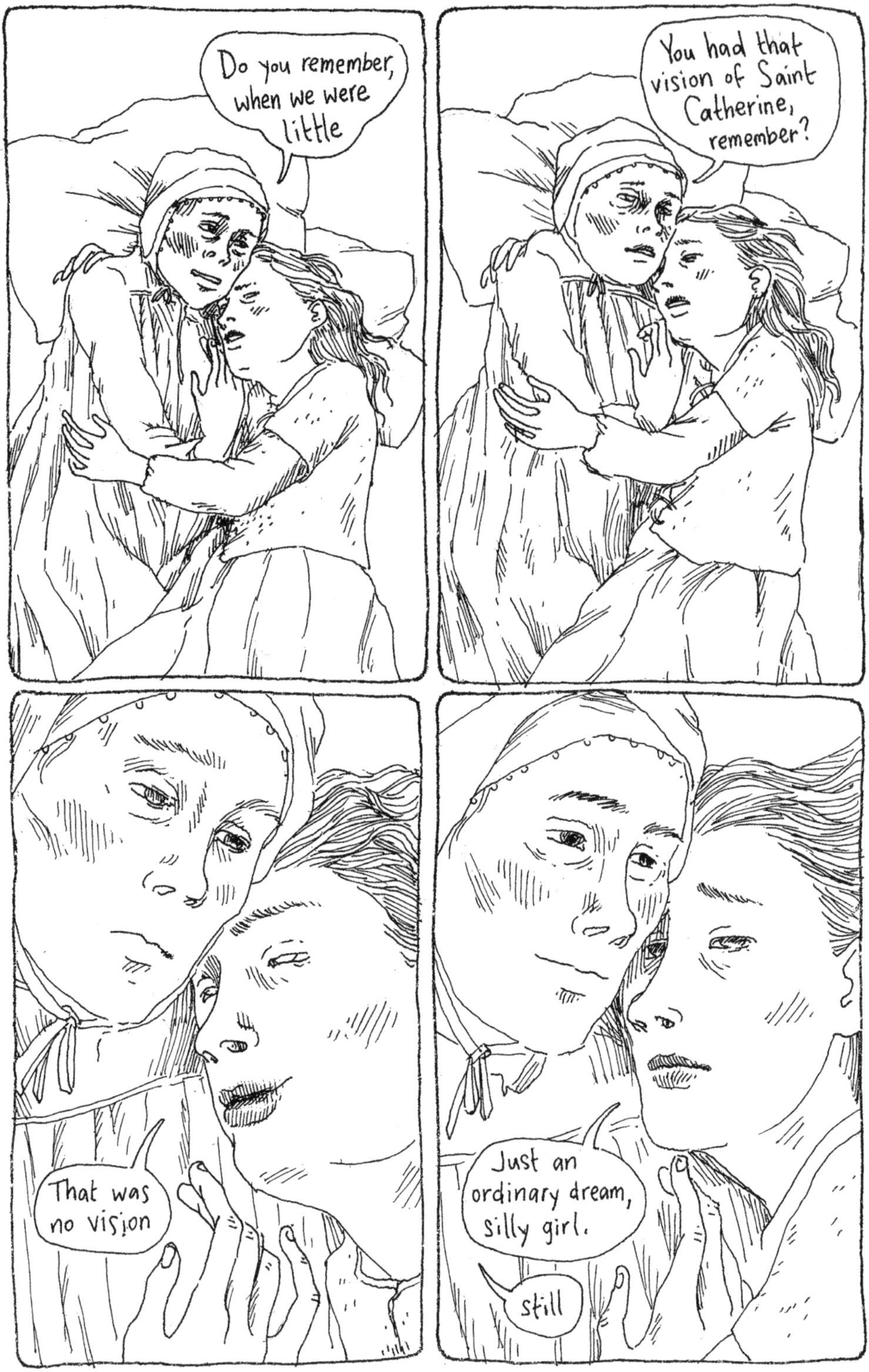
Do you remember, when we were little
You had that vision of Saint Catherine, remember?
That was no vision
Just an ordinary dream, silly girl.
still

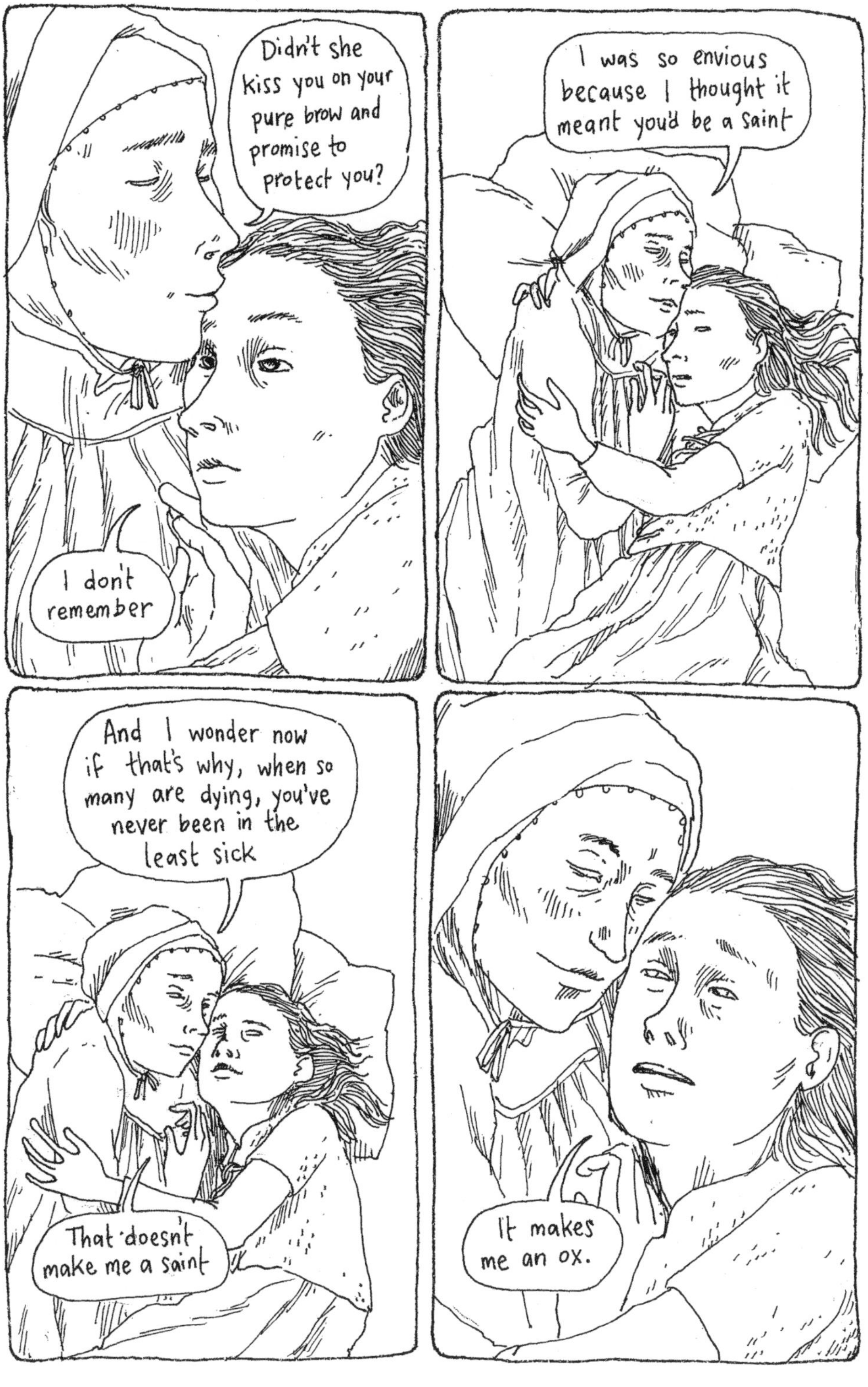
Didn't she kiss you on your pure brow and promise to protect you?
I don't remember
I was so envious because I thought it meant you'd be a saint
And I wonder now if that's why, when so many are dying, you've never been in the least sick
That doesn't make me a saint
It makes me an ox.

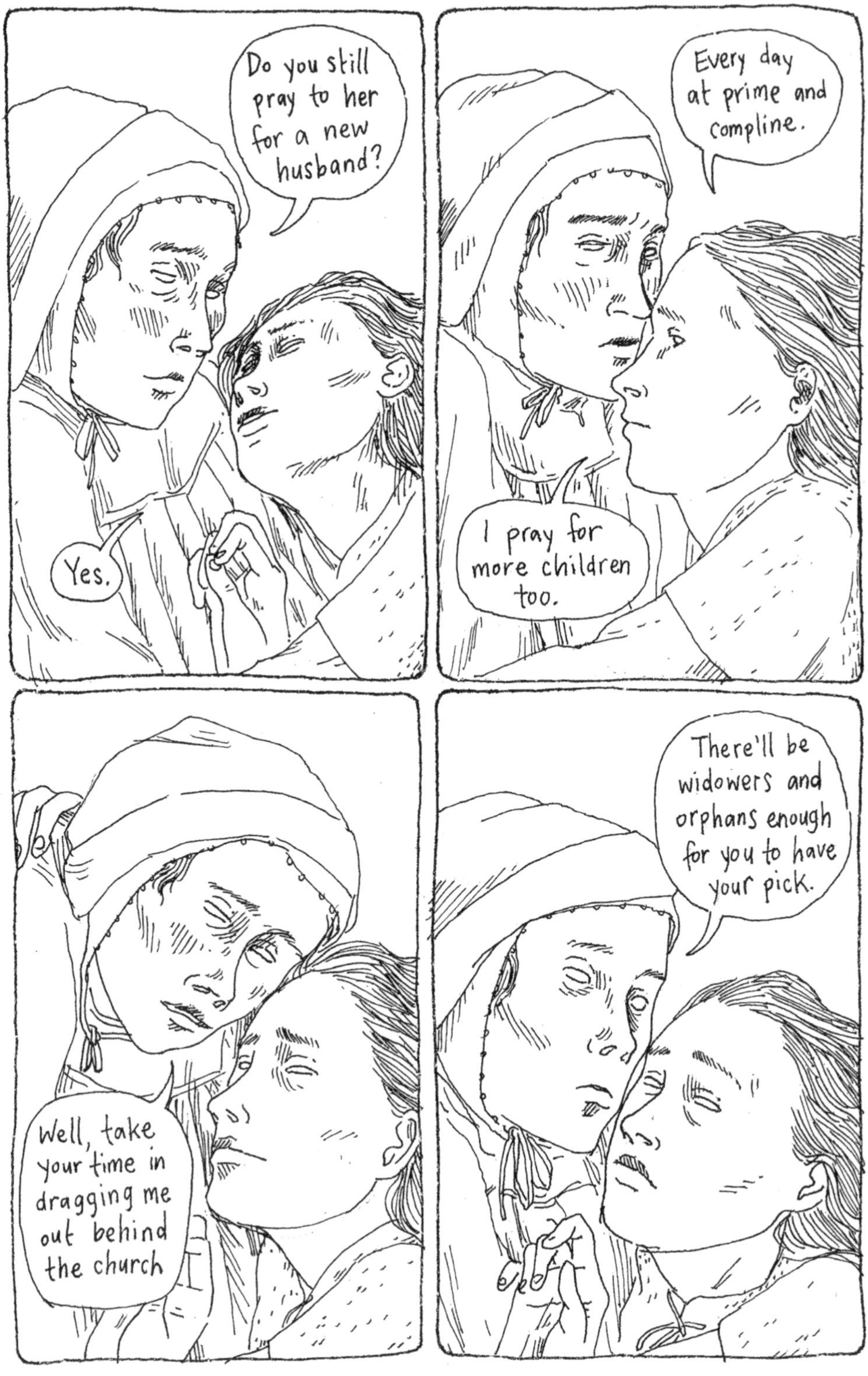
Do you still pray to her for a new husband?
Yes.
Every day at prime and compline.
I pray for more children too.
Well, take your time in dragging me out behind the church
There'll be widowers and orphans enough for you to have your pick.

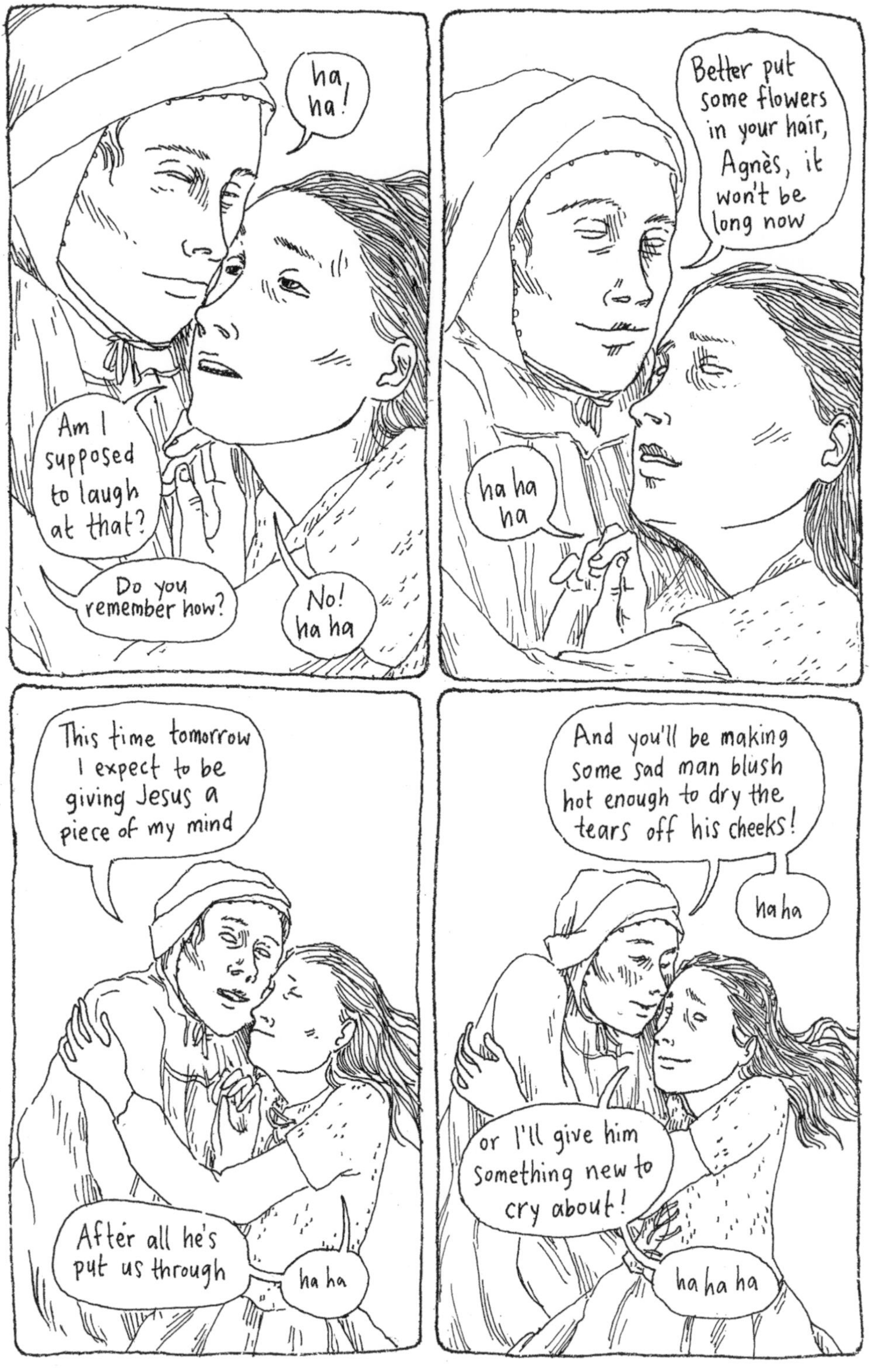
ha, ha!
Am I supposed to laugh at that?
Do you remember how?
No! ha ha
Better put some flowers in your hair, Agnès, it won't be long now
ha ha ha
This time tomorrow I expect to be giving Jesus a piece of my mind
After all he's put us through
ha ha
And you'll be making some sad man blush hot enough to dry the tears off his cheeks!
ha ha
or I'll give him something new to cry about!
ha ha ha

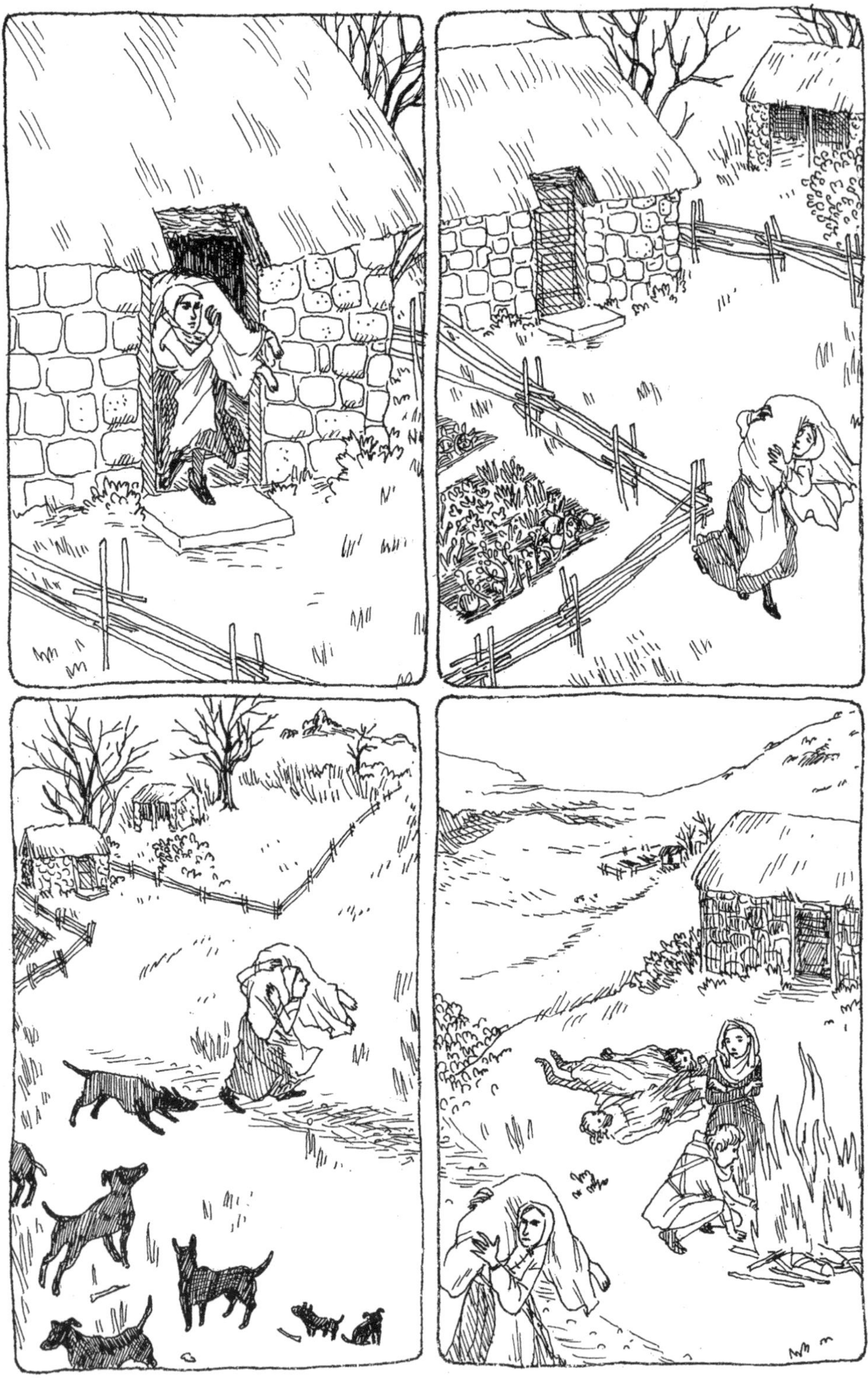

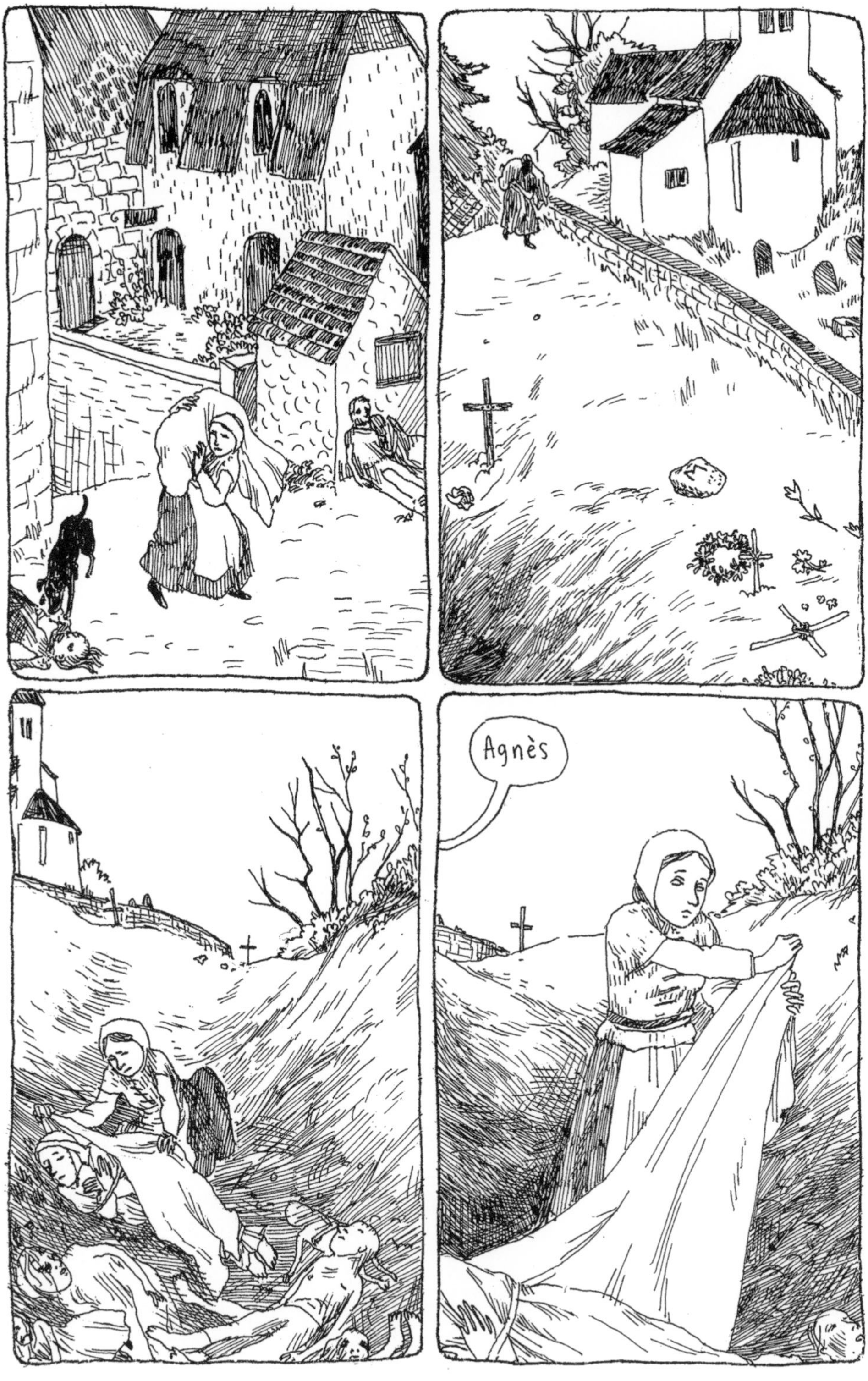
Agnès

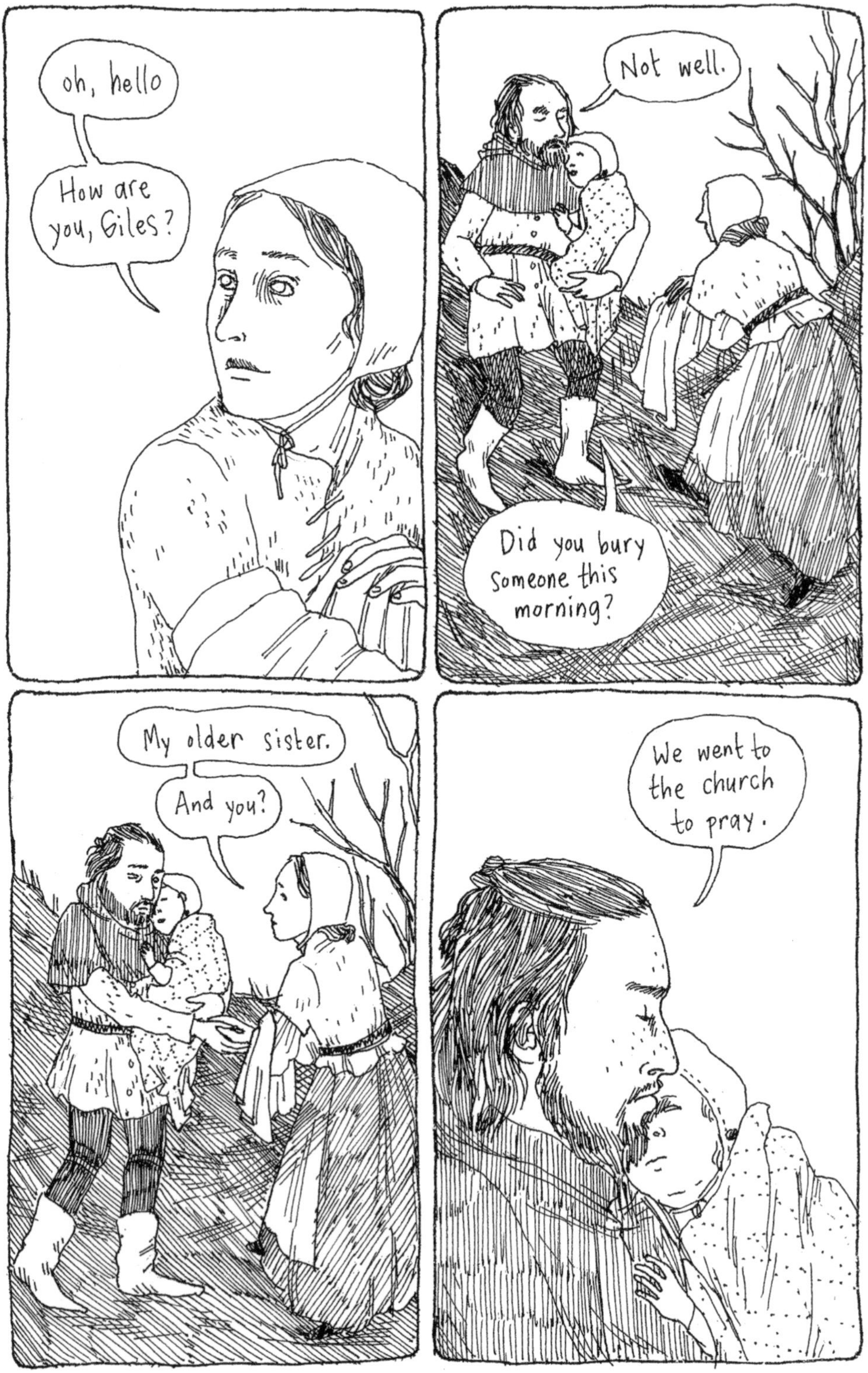
oh, hello
How are you, Giles?
Not well.
Did you bury someone this morning?
My older sister.
And you?
We went to the church to pray.

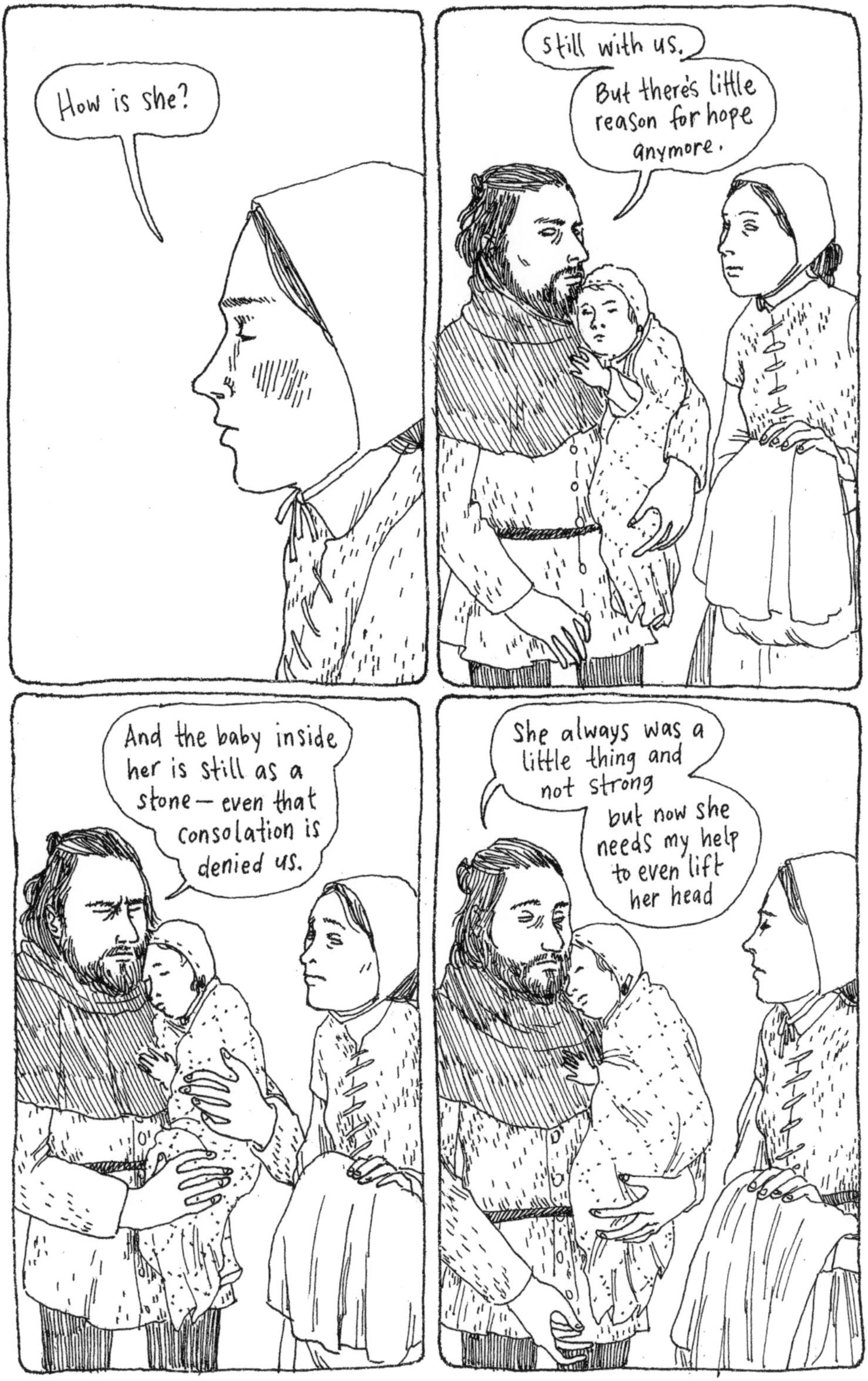
How is she?
Still with us.
But there's little reason for hope anymore.
And the baby inside her is still as a stone— even that consolation is denied us.
She always was a little thing and not strong
but now she needs my help to even lift her head

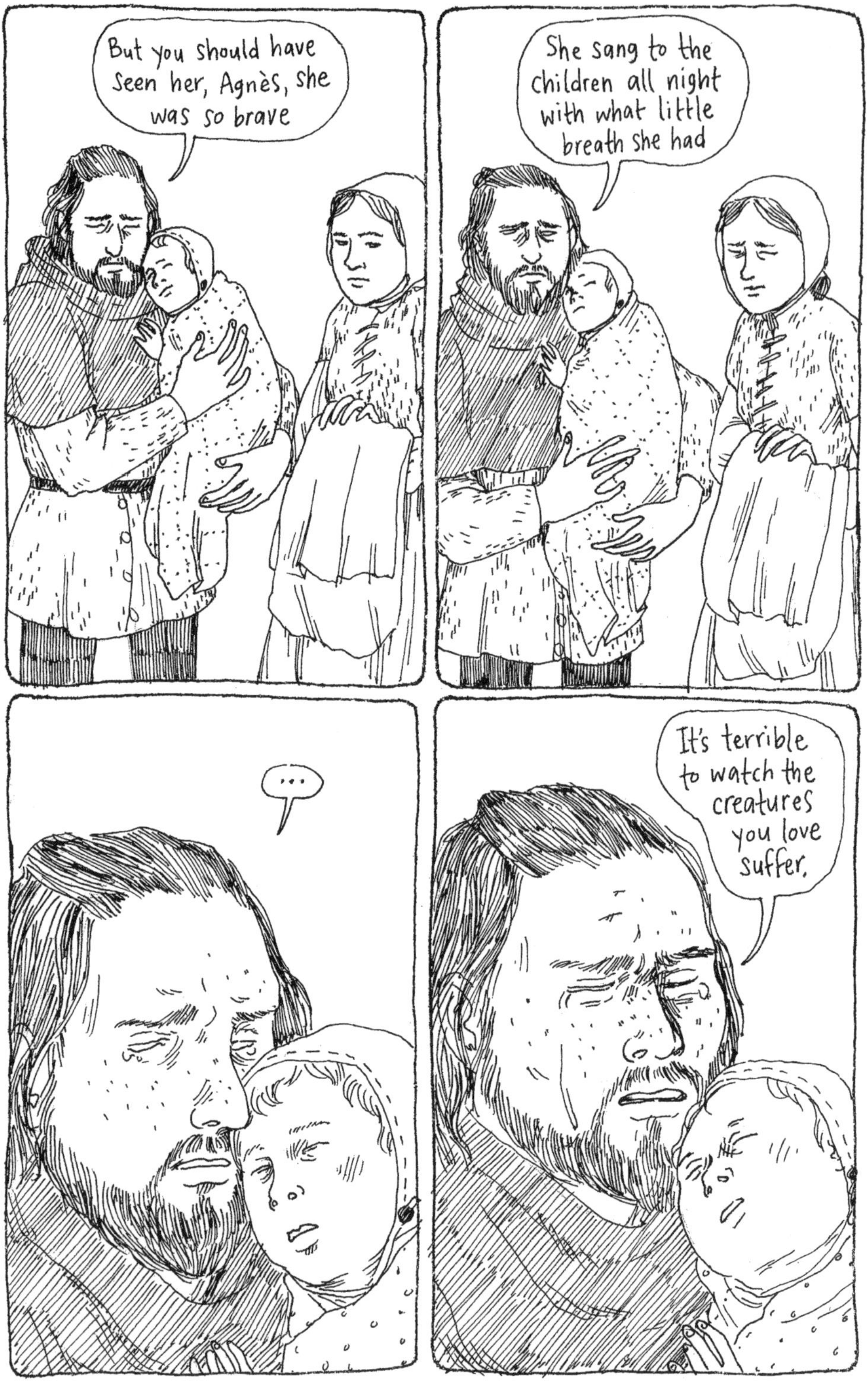
But you should have seen her, Agnès, she was so brave
She sang to the children all night with what little breath she had
...
It's terrible to watch the creatures you love suffer.

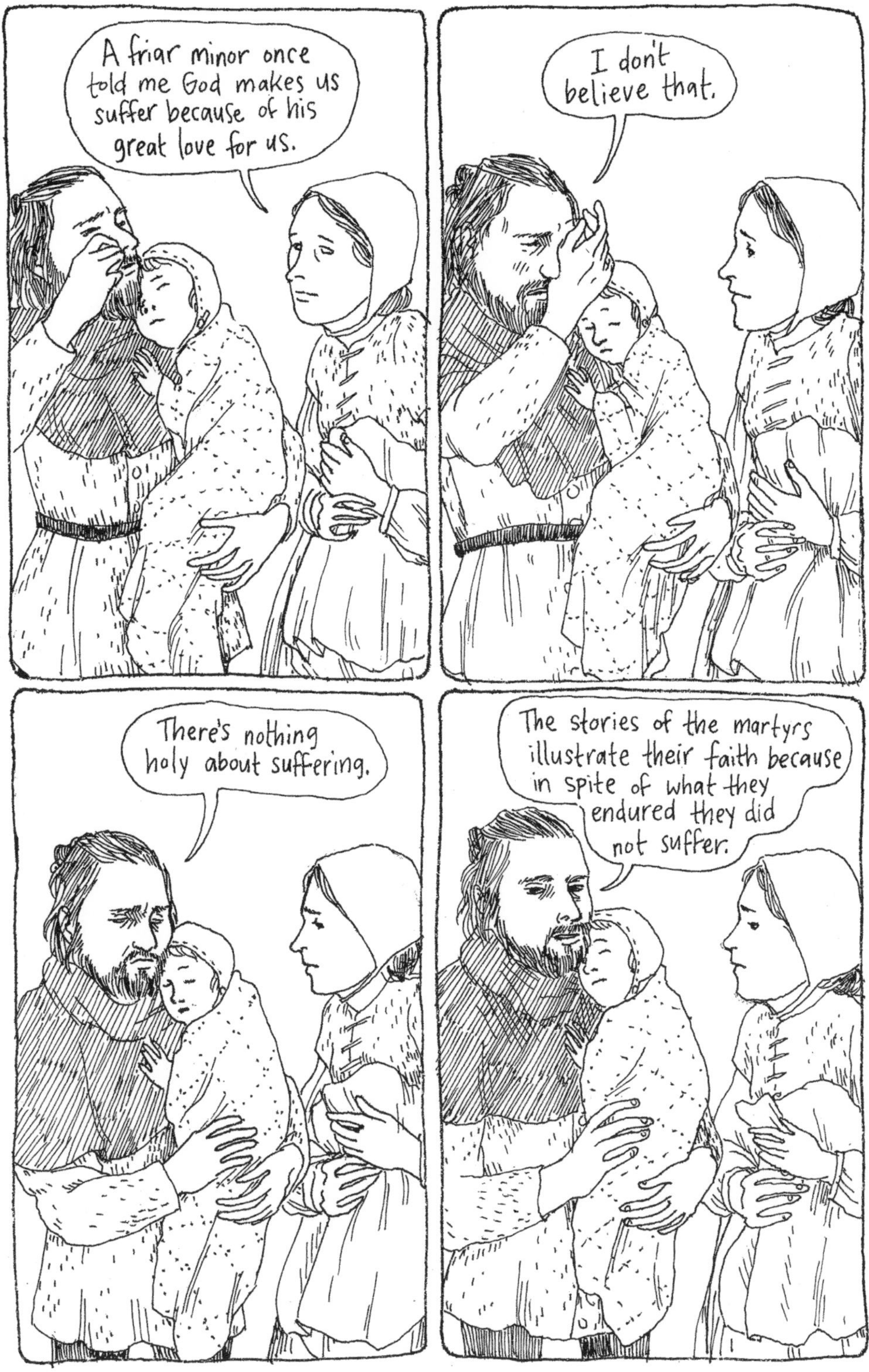
A friar minor once told me God makes us suffer because of his great love for us.
I don't believe that.
There's nothing holy about suffering.
The stories of the martyrs illustrate their faith because in spite of what they endured they did not suffer.

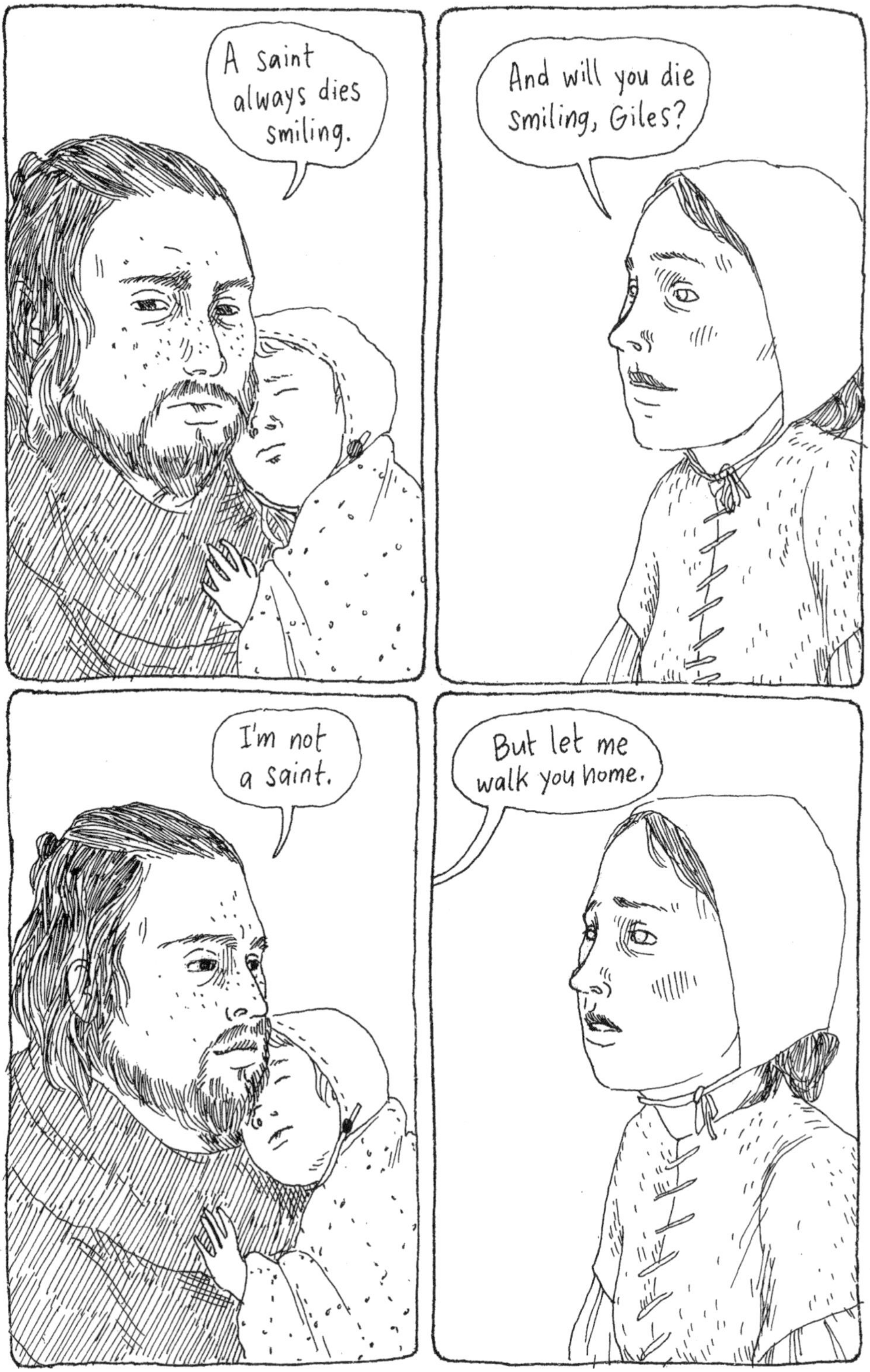
A saint always dies smiling.
And will you die smiling, Giles?
I'm not a saint.
But let me walk you home.

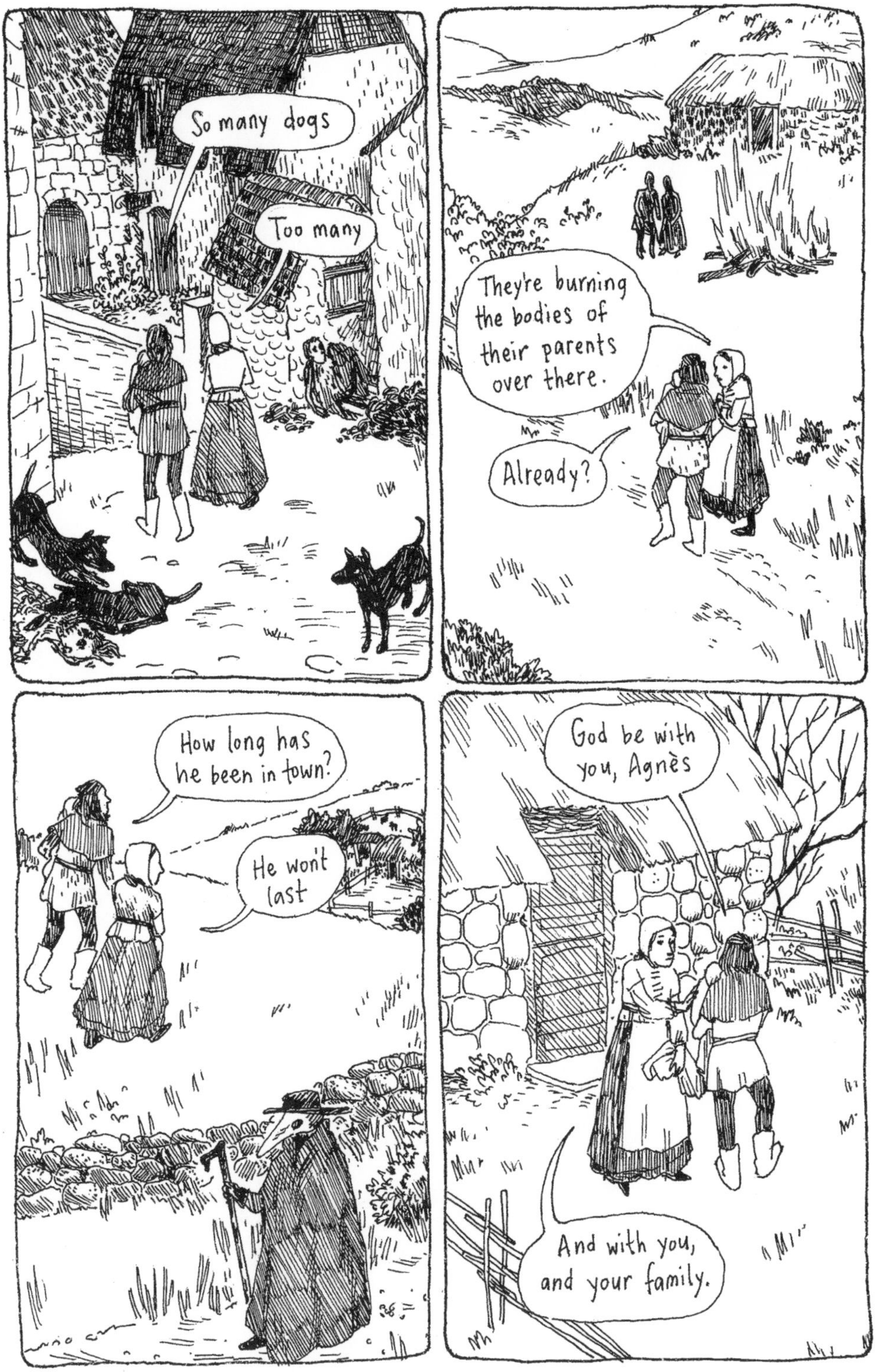
So many dogs
Too many
They're burning the bodies of their parents over there.
Already?
How long has he been in town?
He won't last
God be with you, Agnès
And with you, and your family.

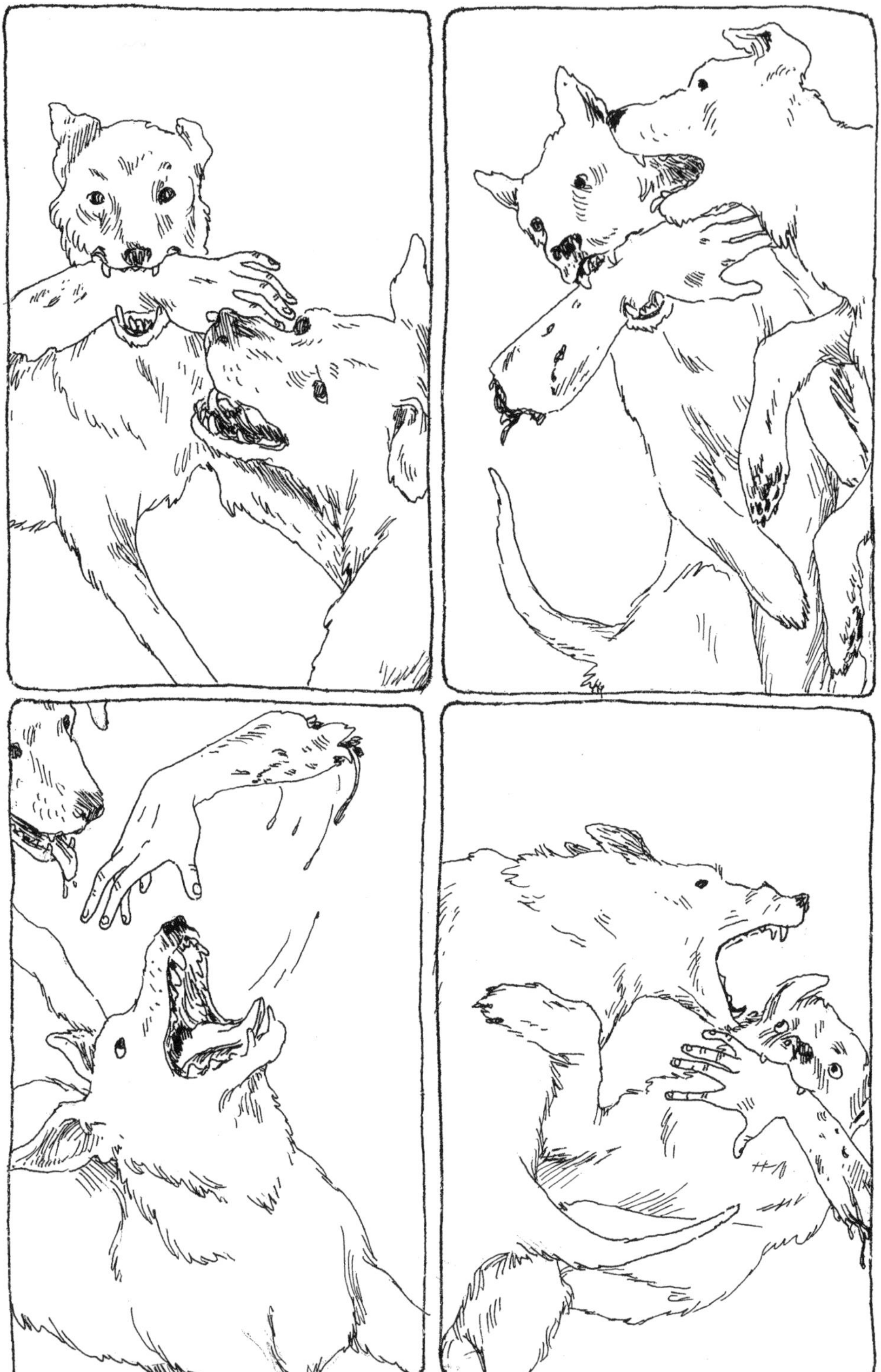

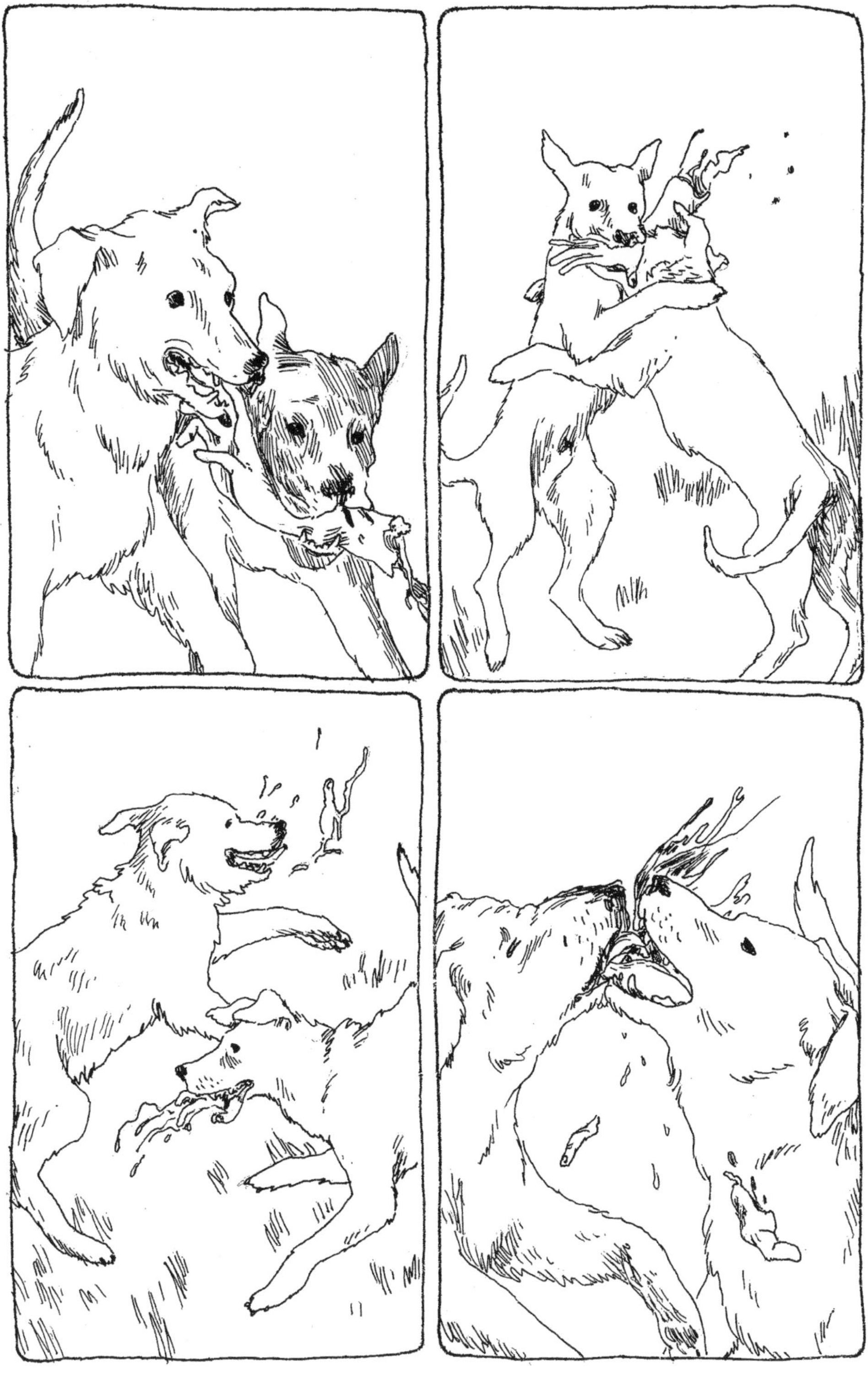

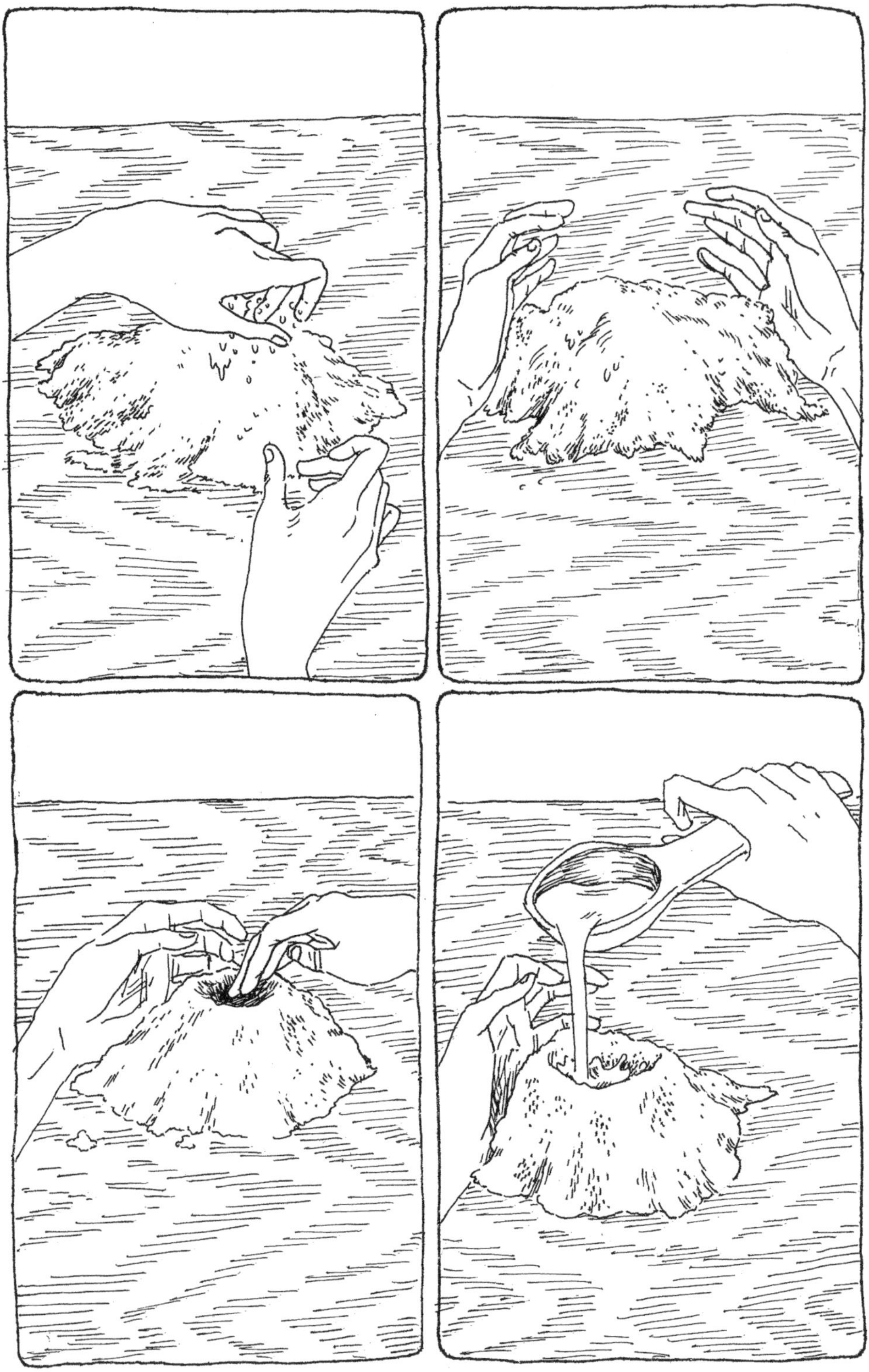

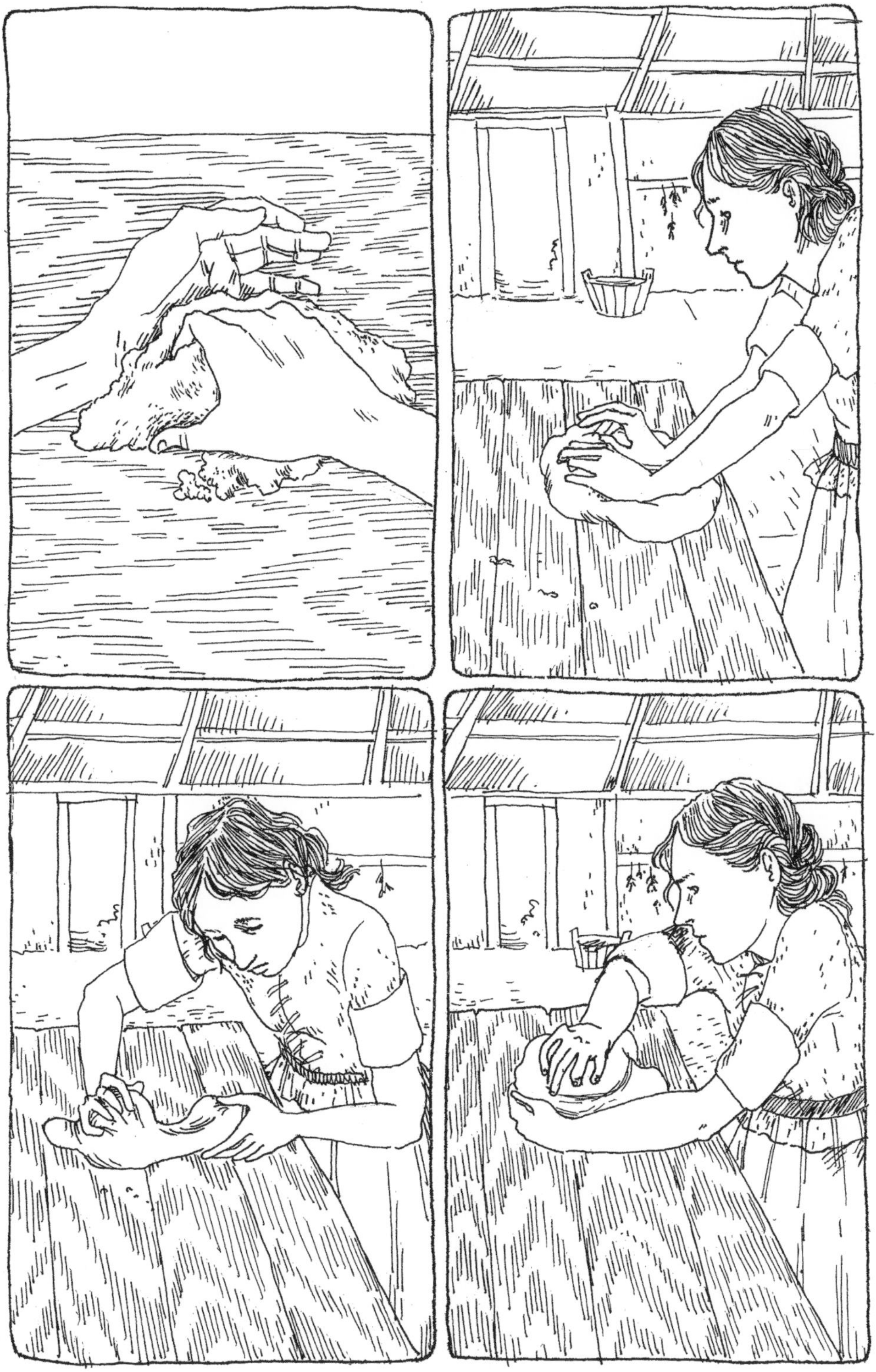

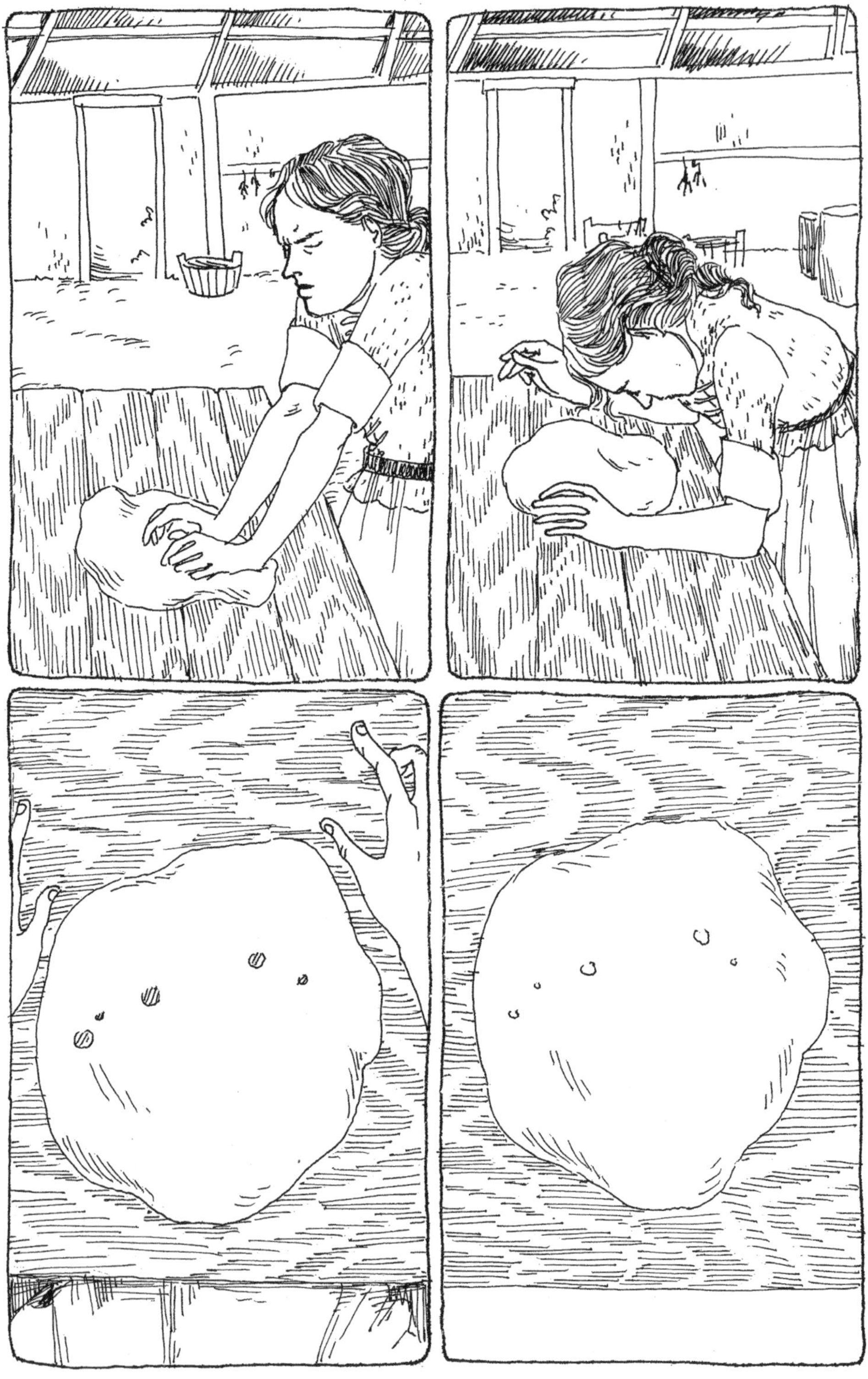

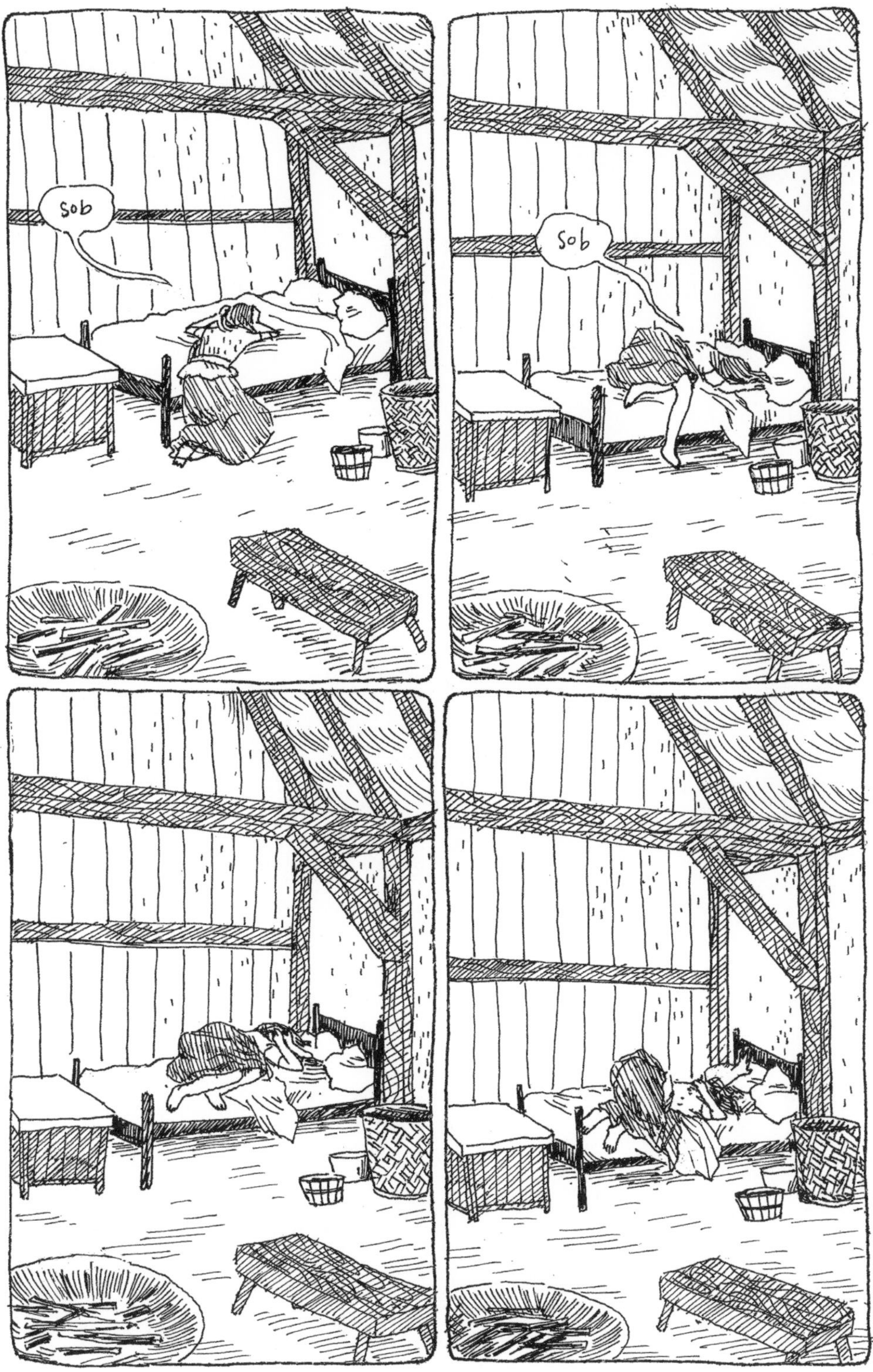
sob
sob

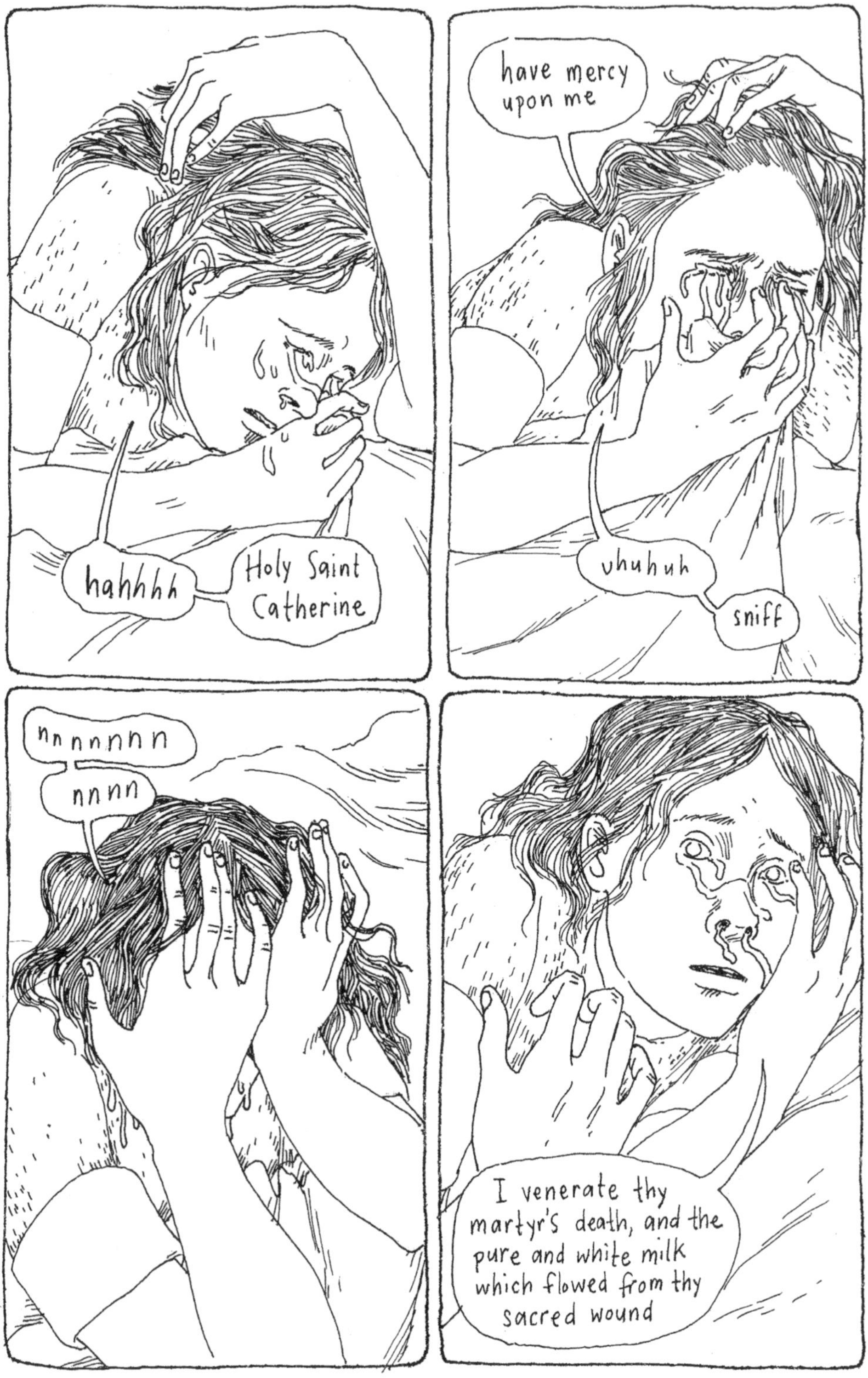
hahhhh
Holy Saint Catherine
have mercy upon me
uhuhuh
sniff
nnnnnnn
nnnn
I venerate thy martyr's death, and the pure and white milk which flowed from thy sacred wound

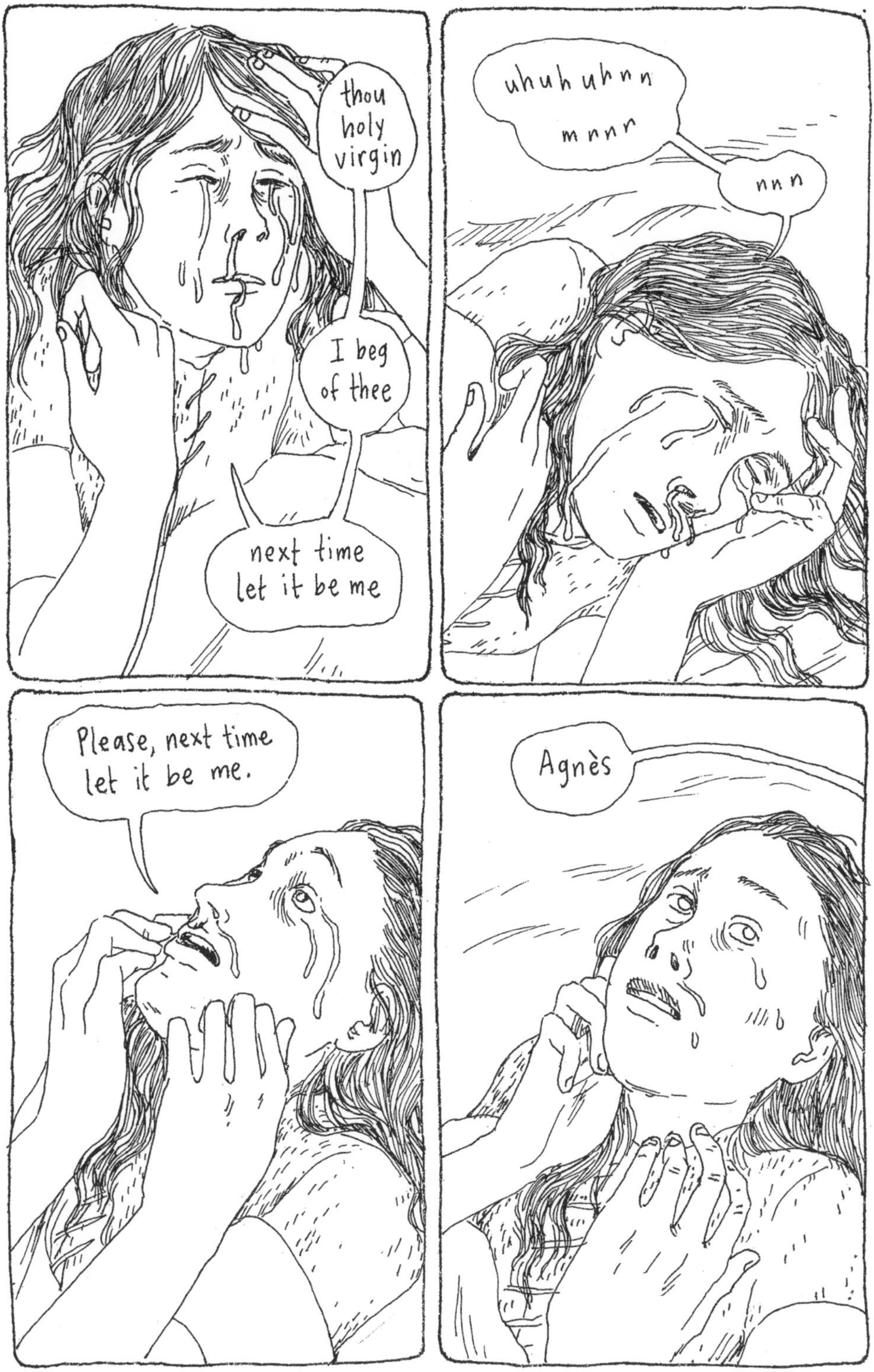
thou holy virgin
I beg of thee
next time let it be me
uhuh uhnn mnnr
nnn
Please, next time let it be me.
Agnès

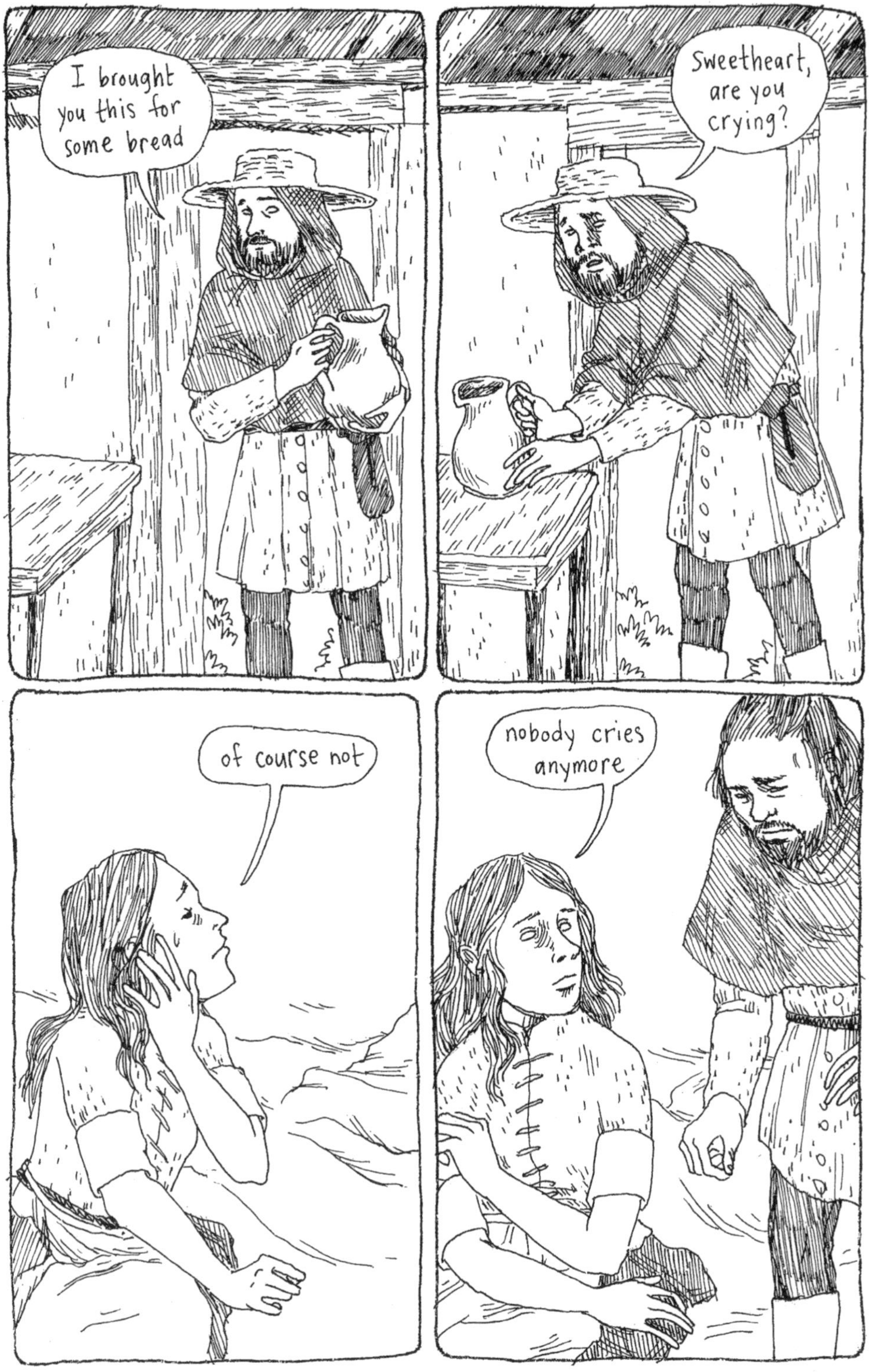
I brought you this for some bread
Sweetheart, are you crying?
of course not
nobody cries anymore

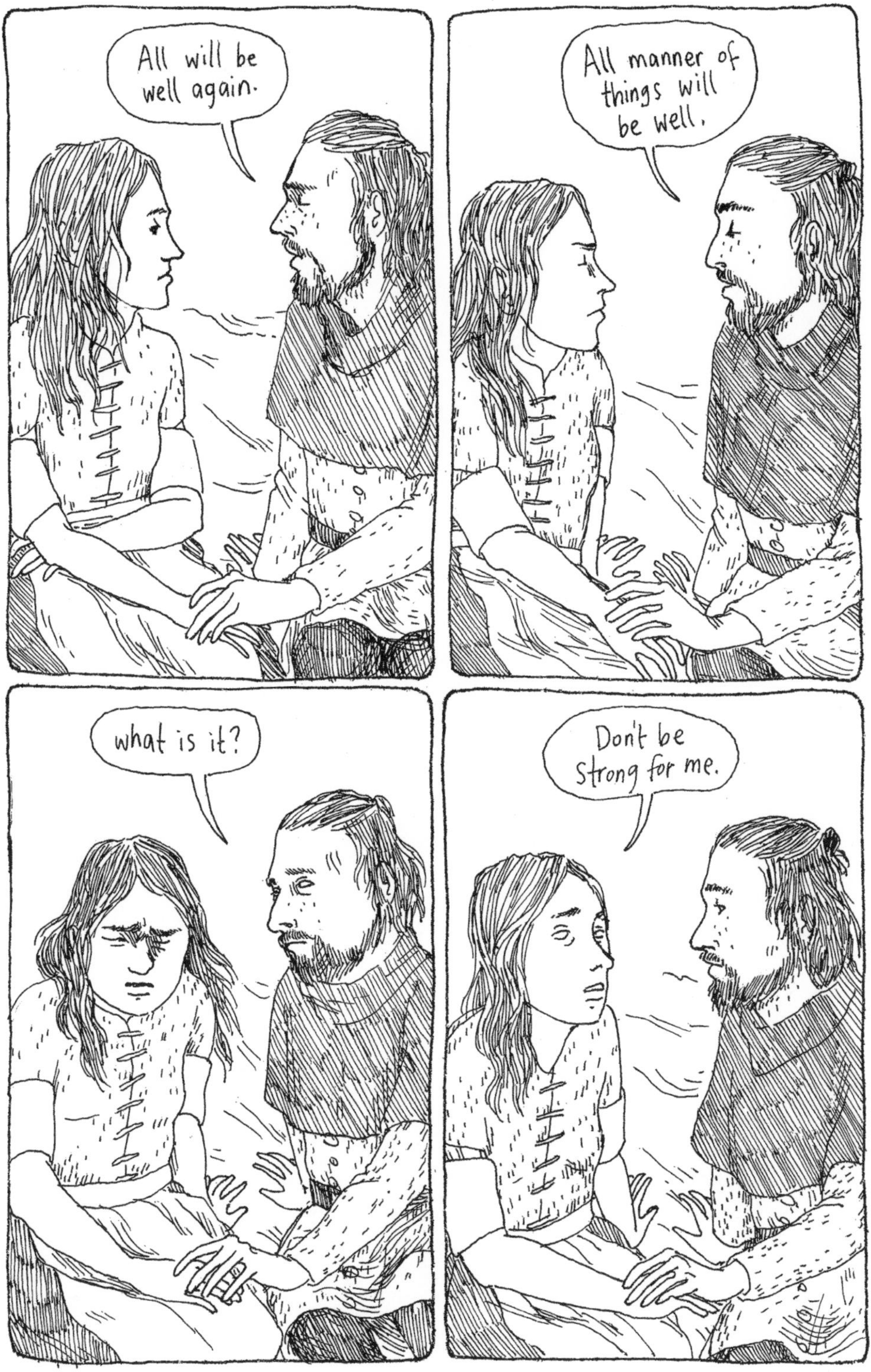
All will be well again.
All manner of things will be well.
what is it?
Don't be strong for me.

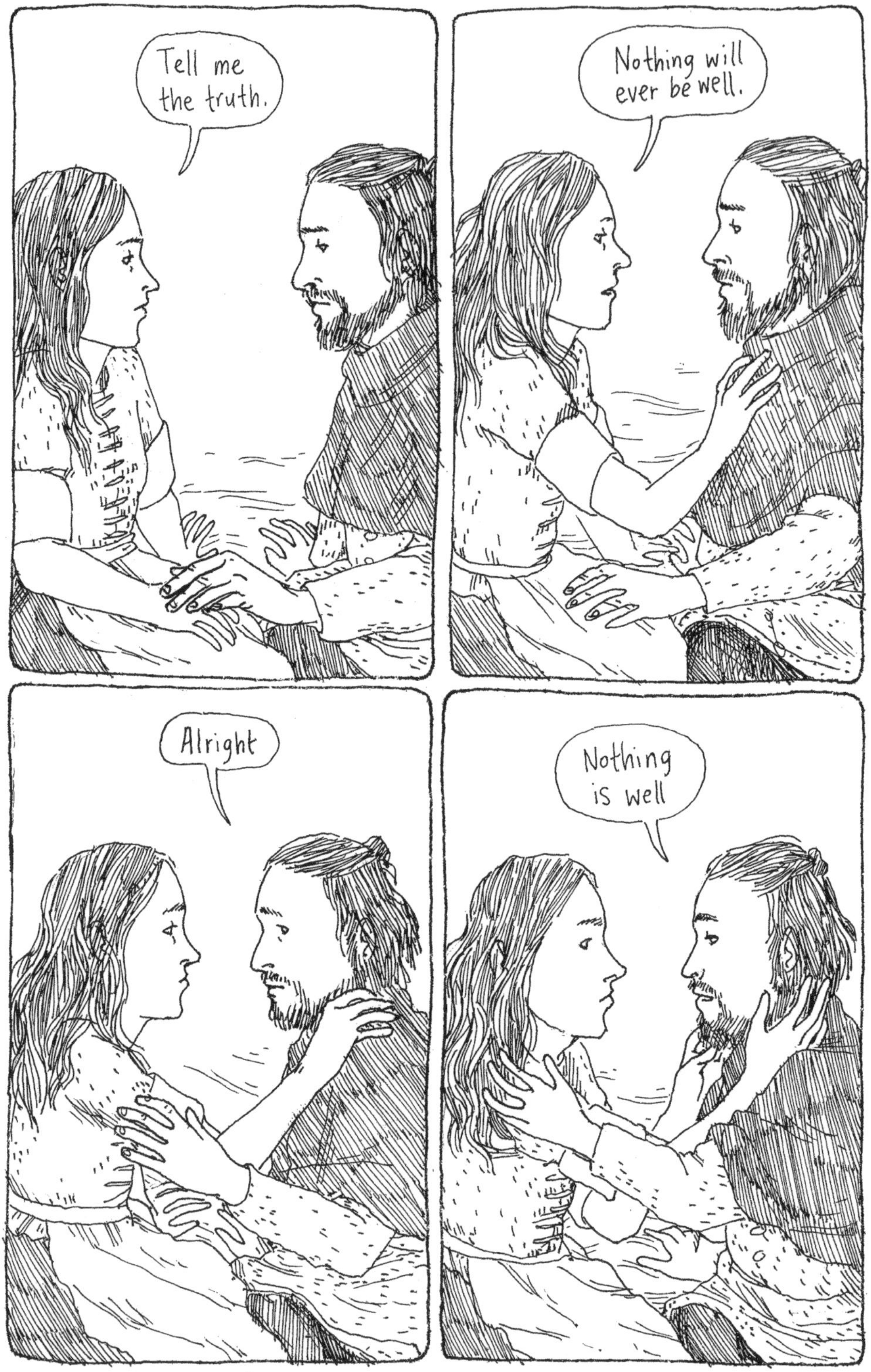
Tell me the truth.
Nothing will ever be well.
Alright
Nothing is well

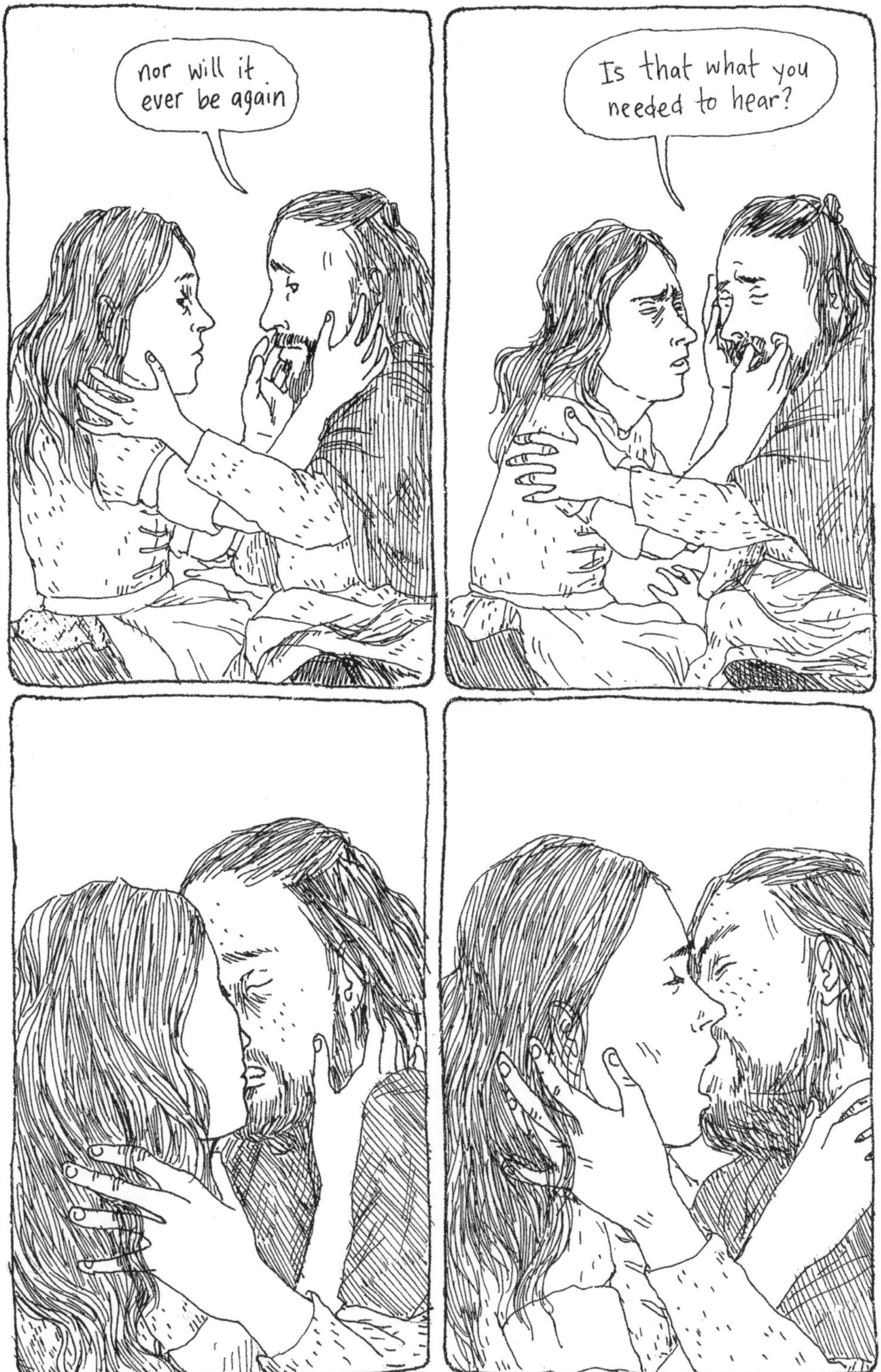
nor will it ever be again
Is that what you needed to hear?

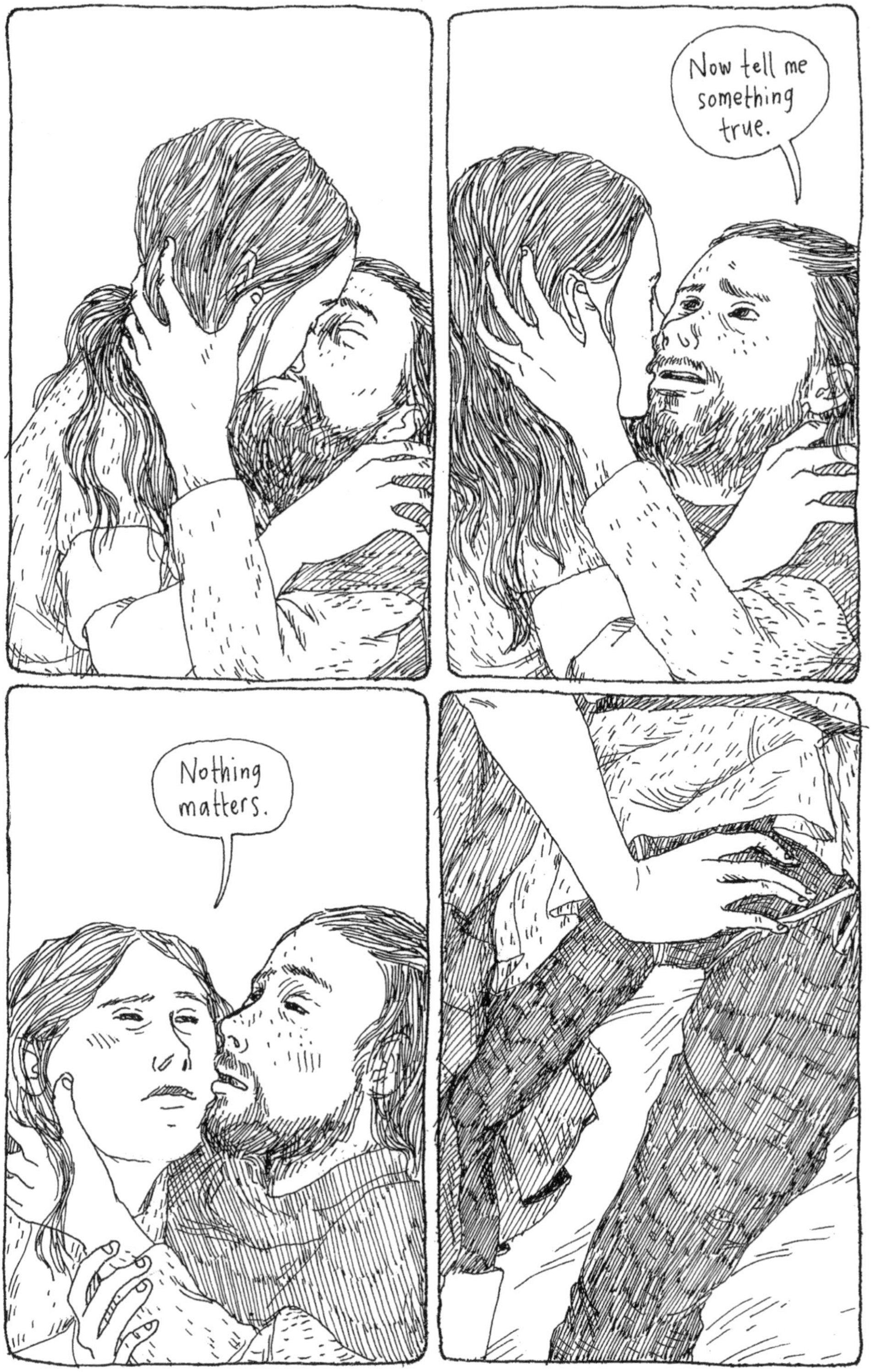
Now tell me something true.
Nothing matters.

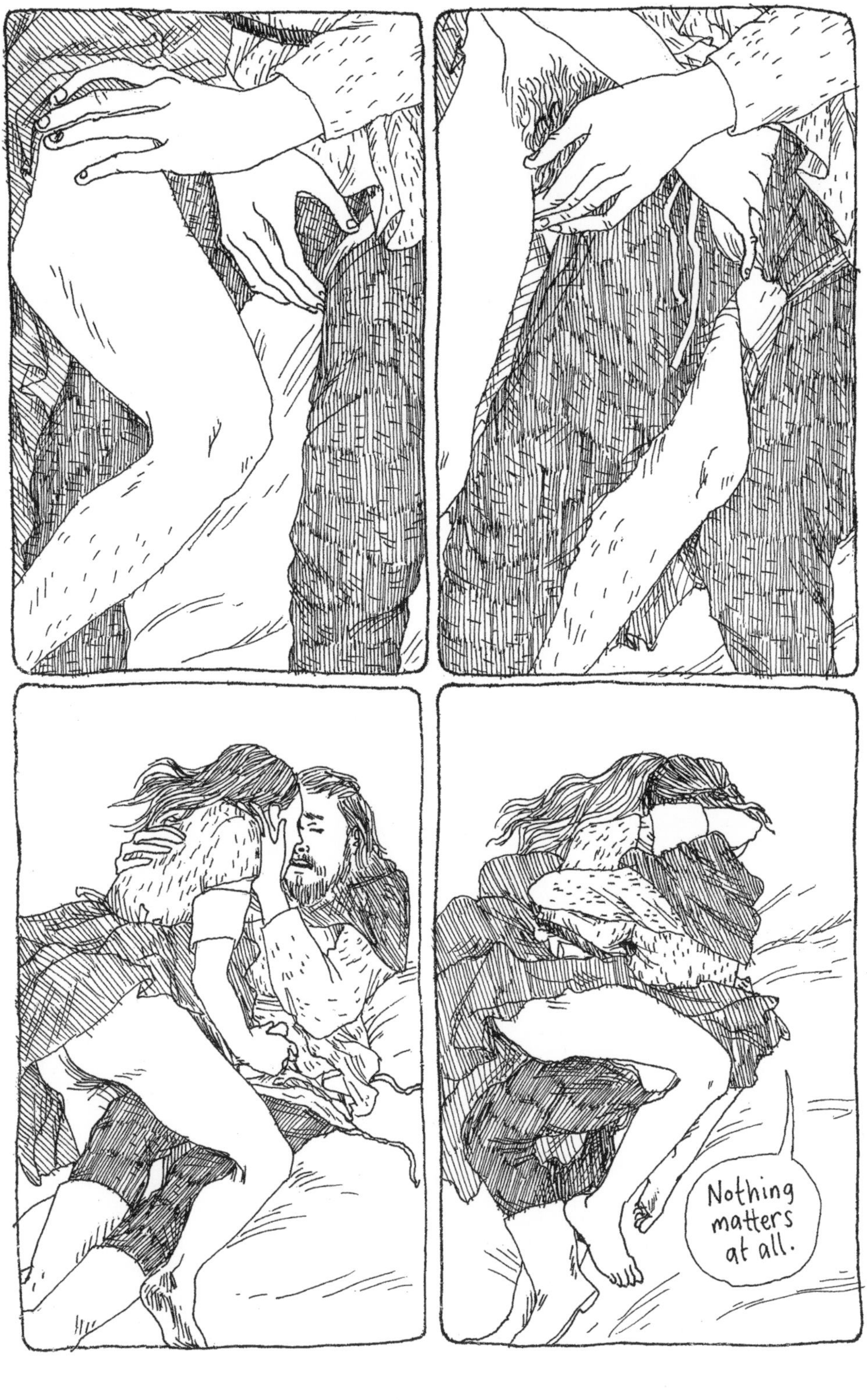
Nothing matters at all.

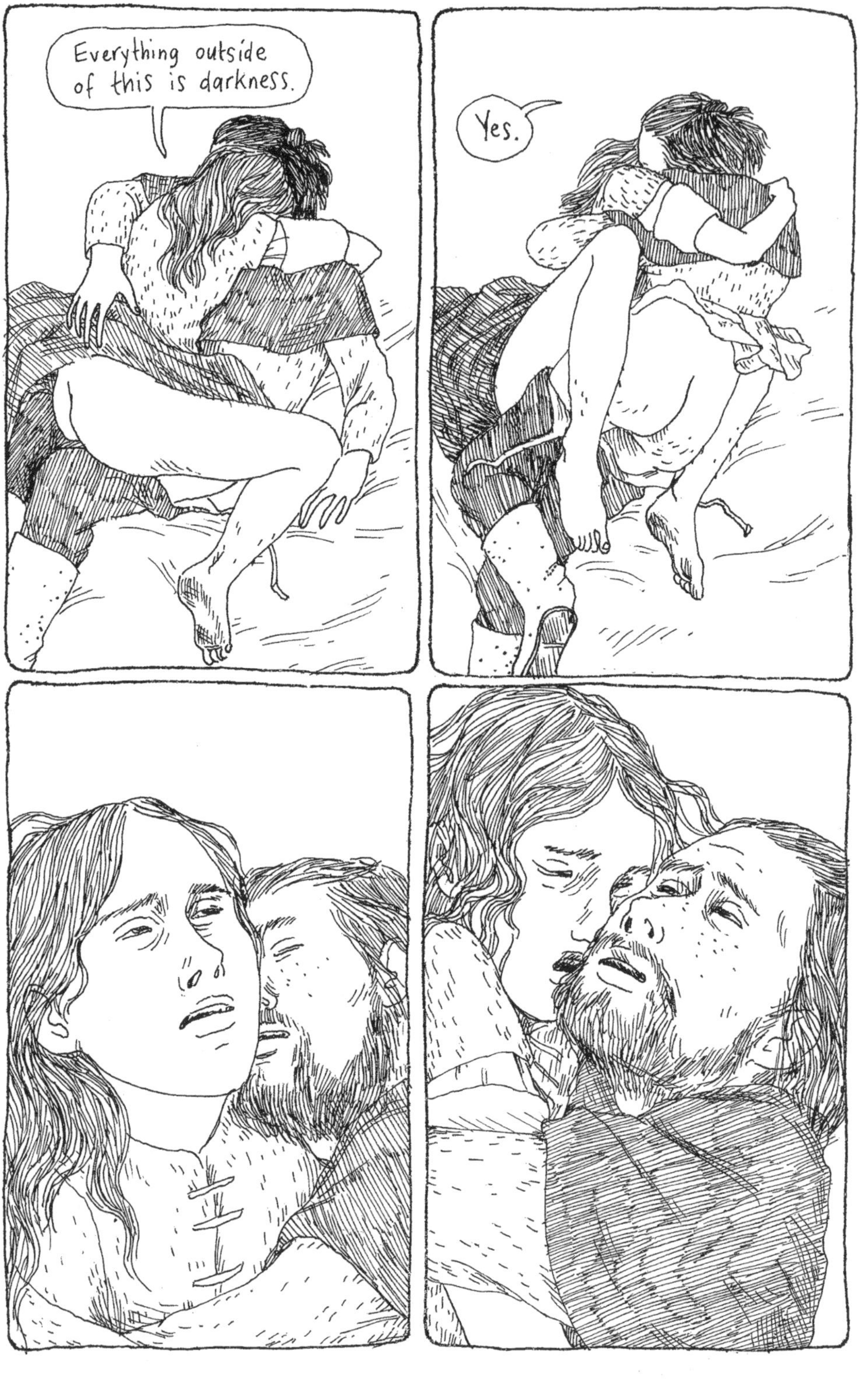
Everything outside of this is darkness.
Yes.

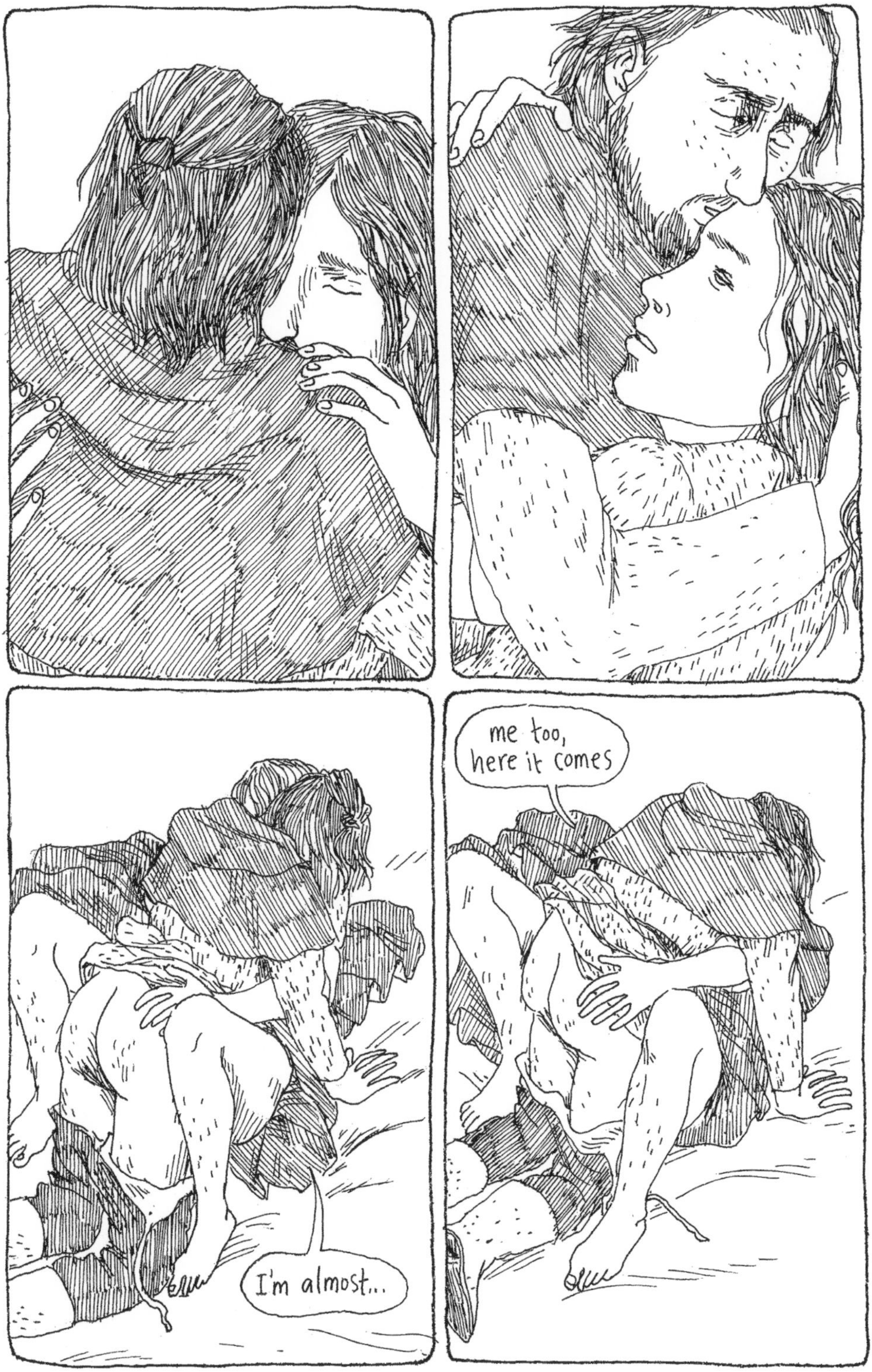
I'm almost...
me too, here it comes

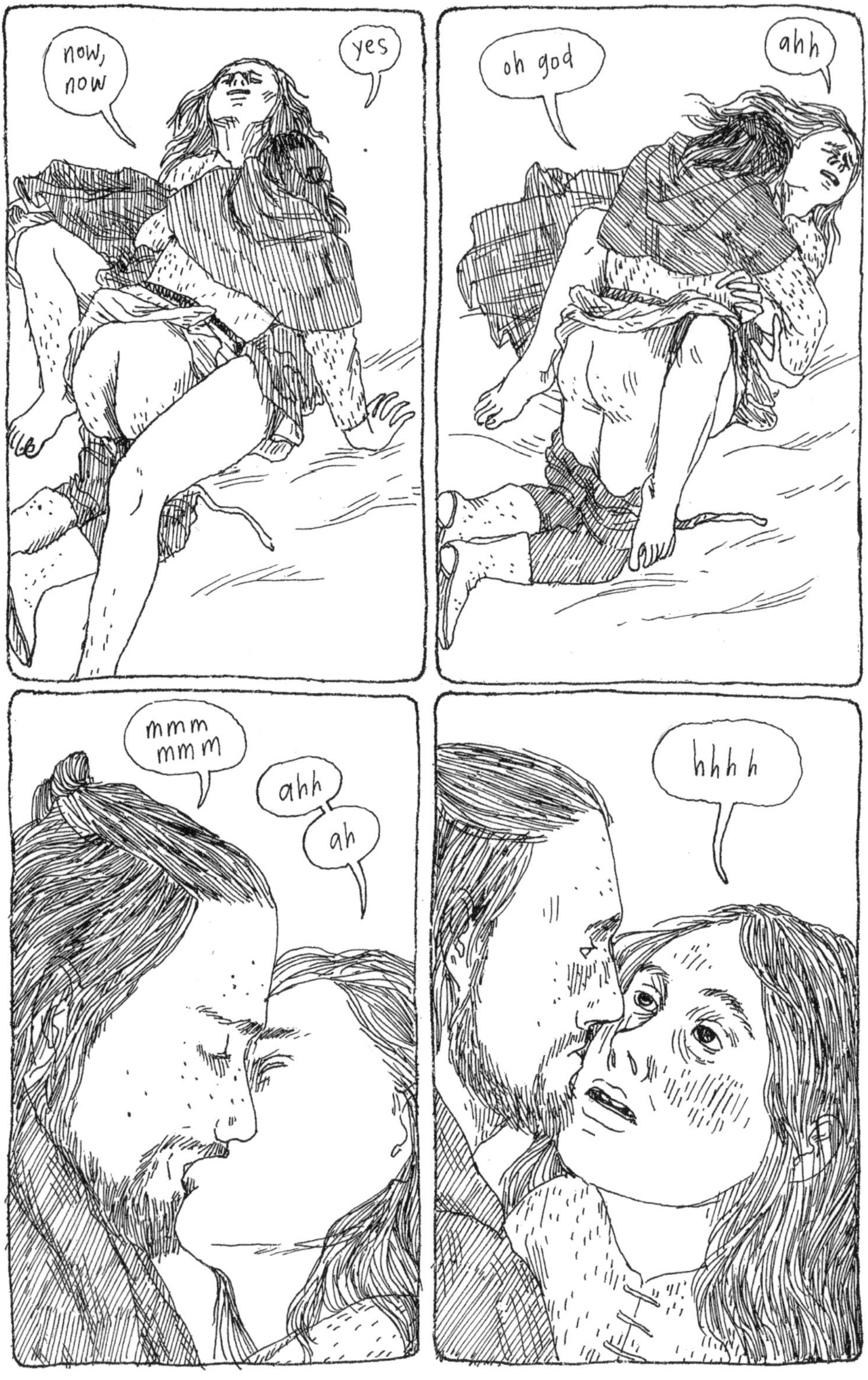
now,
now
yes
oh god
ahh
mmm
mmm
ahh
ah
hhhh

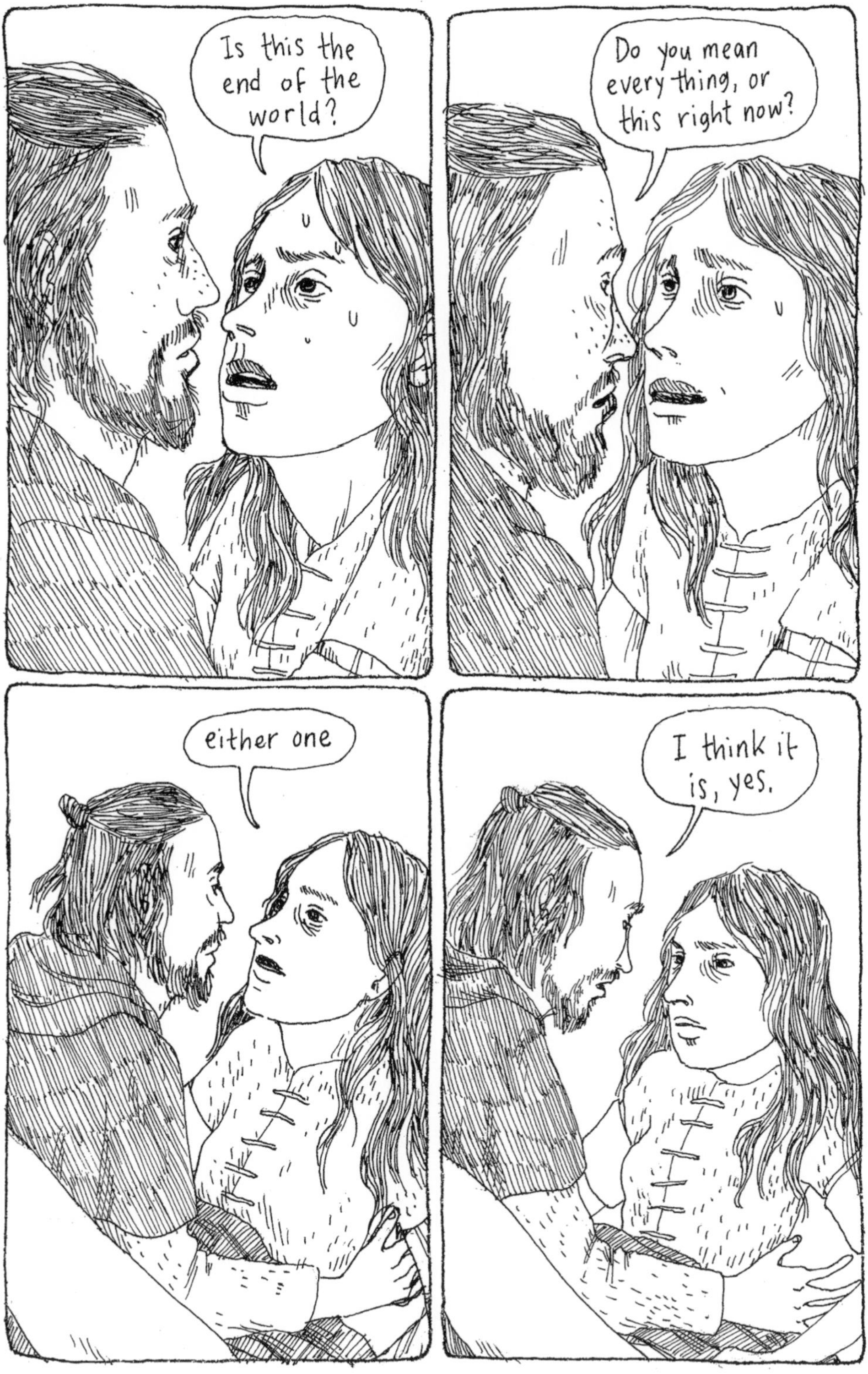
Is this the end of the world?
Do you mean every thing, or this right now?
either one
I think it is, yes.

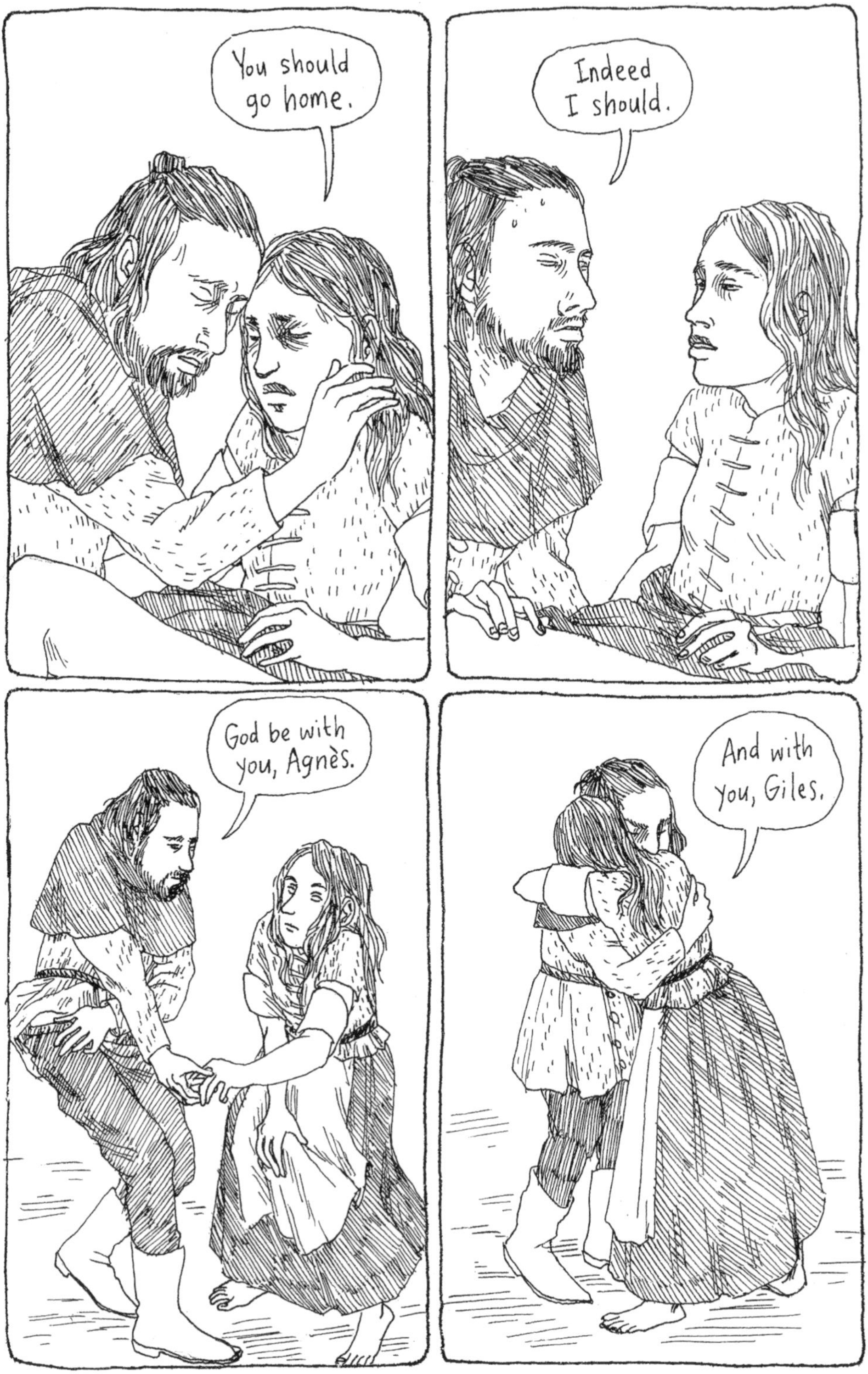
You should go home.
Indeed I should.
God be with you, Agnès.
And with you, Giles.

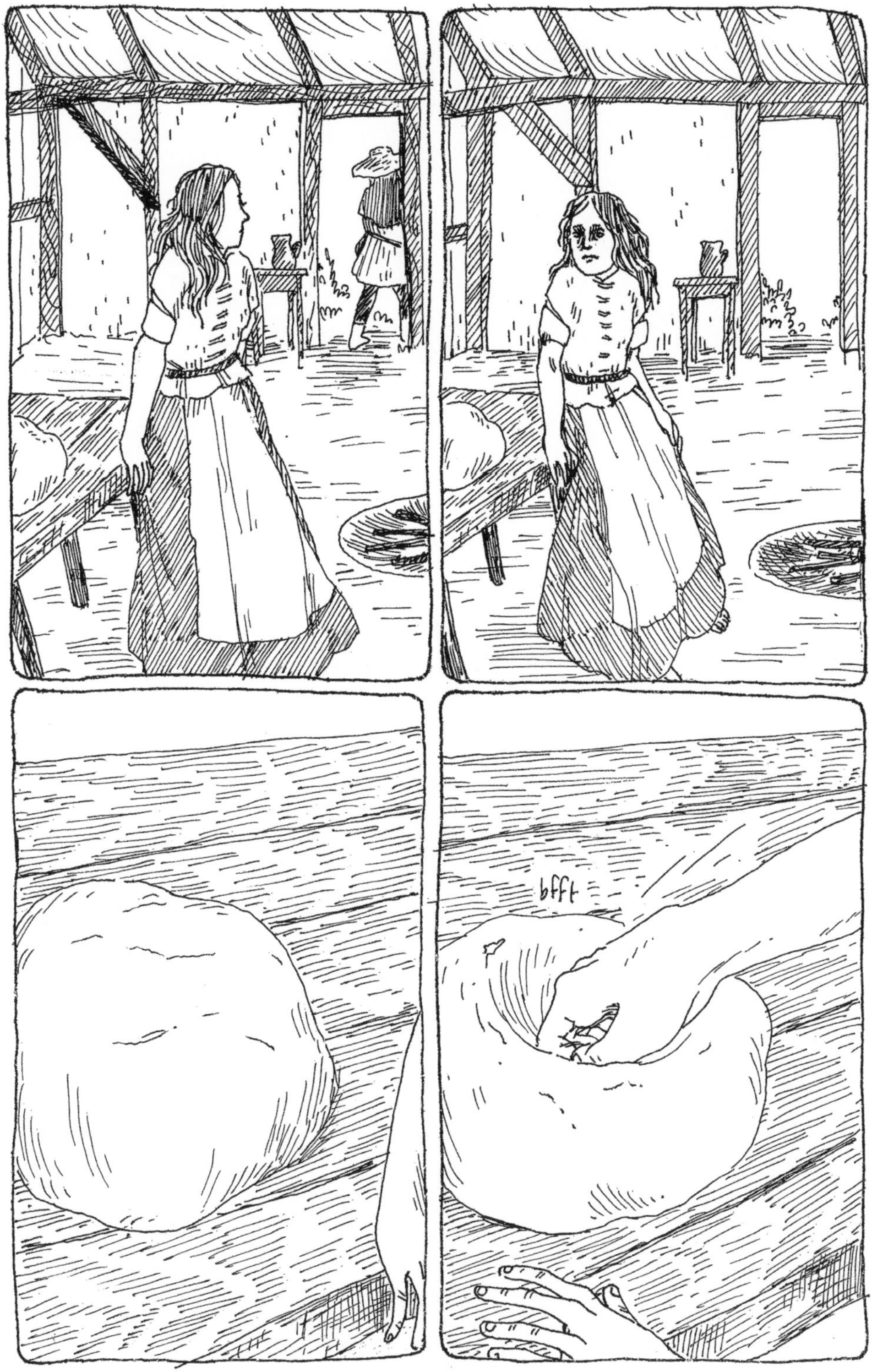
bfft

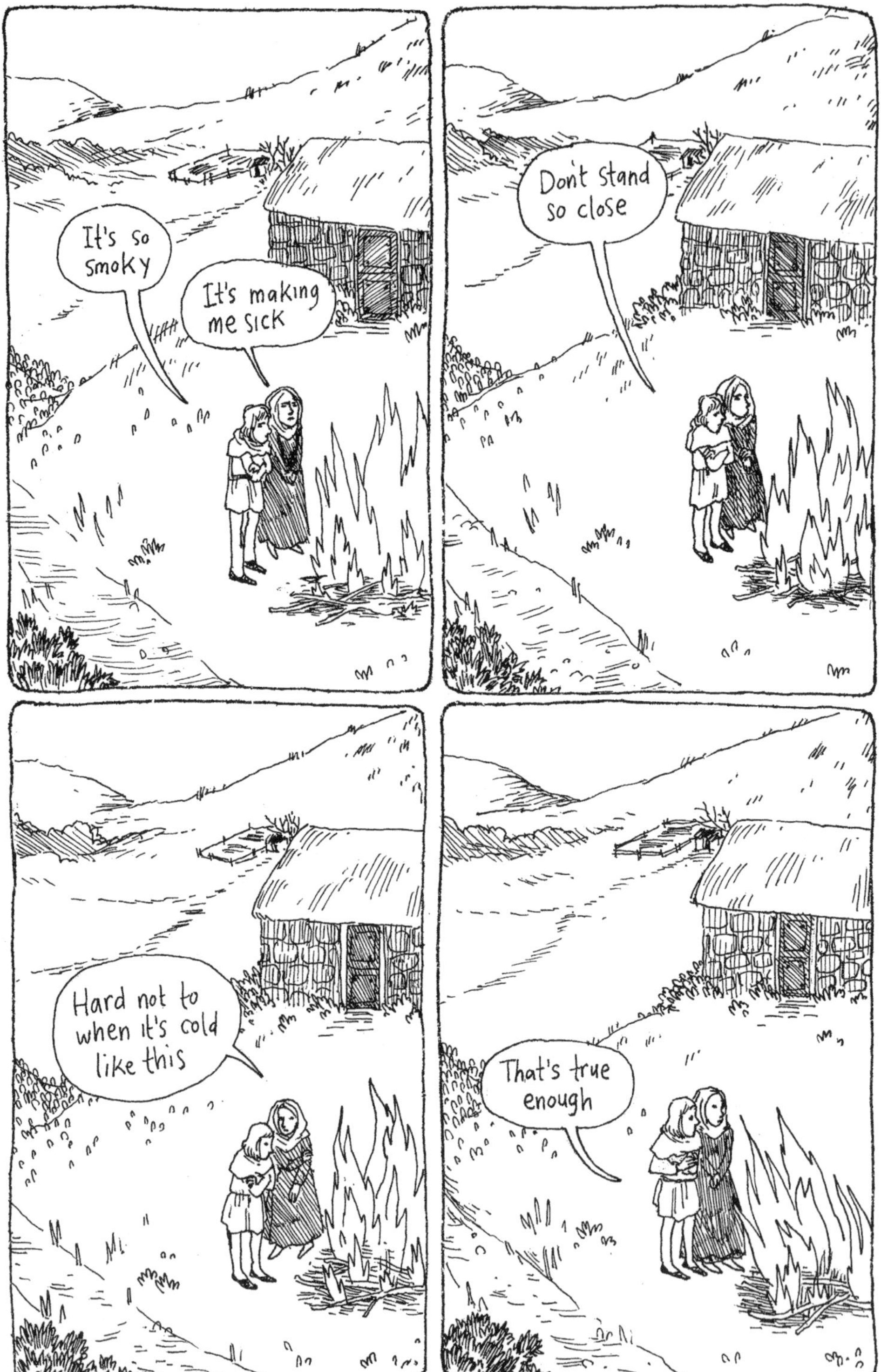
It's so smoky
It's making me sick
Don't stand so close
Hard not to when it's cold like this
That's true enough

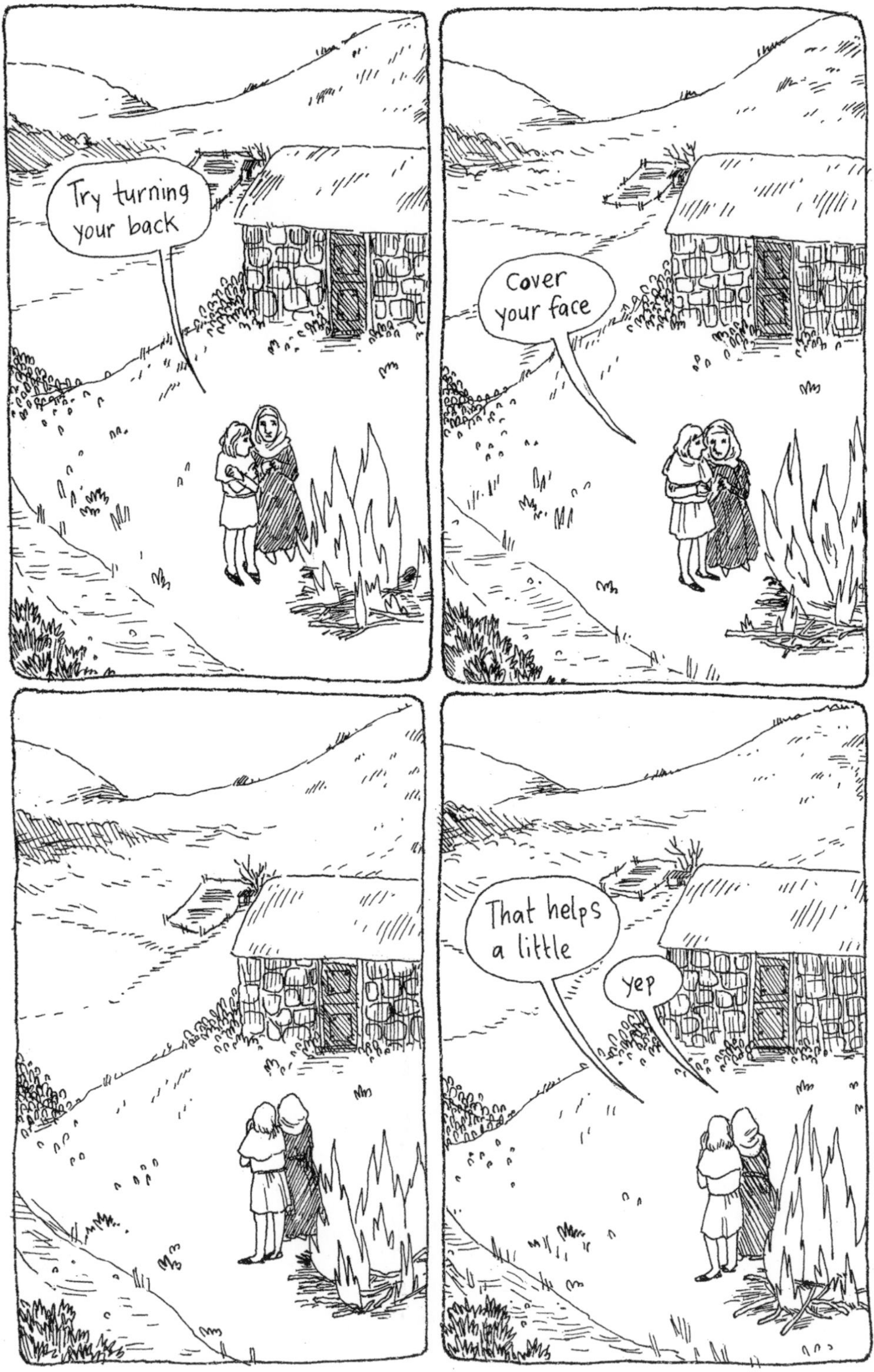
Try turning your back
Cover your face
That helps a little
yep

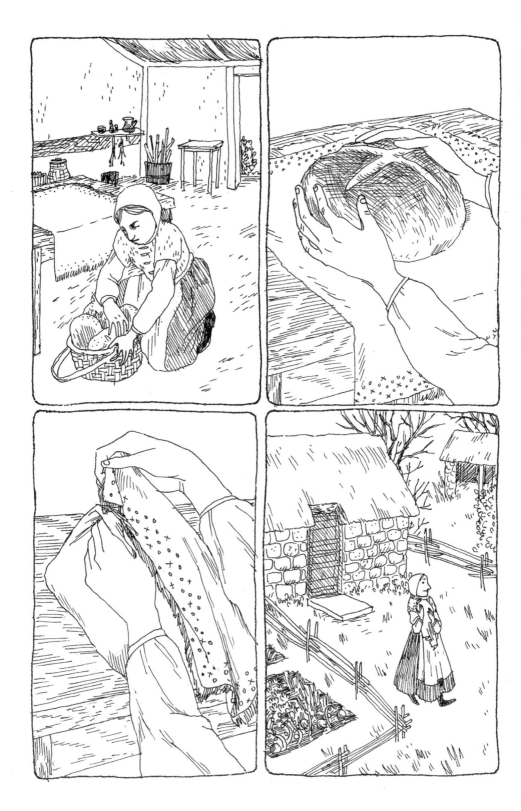

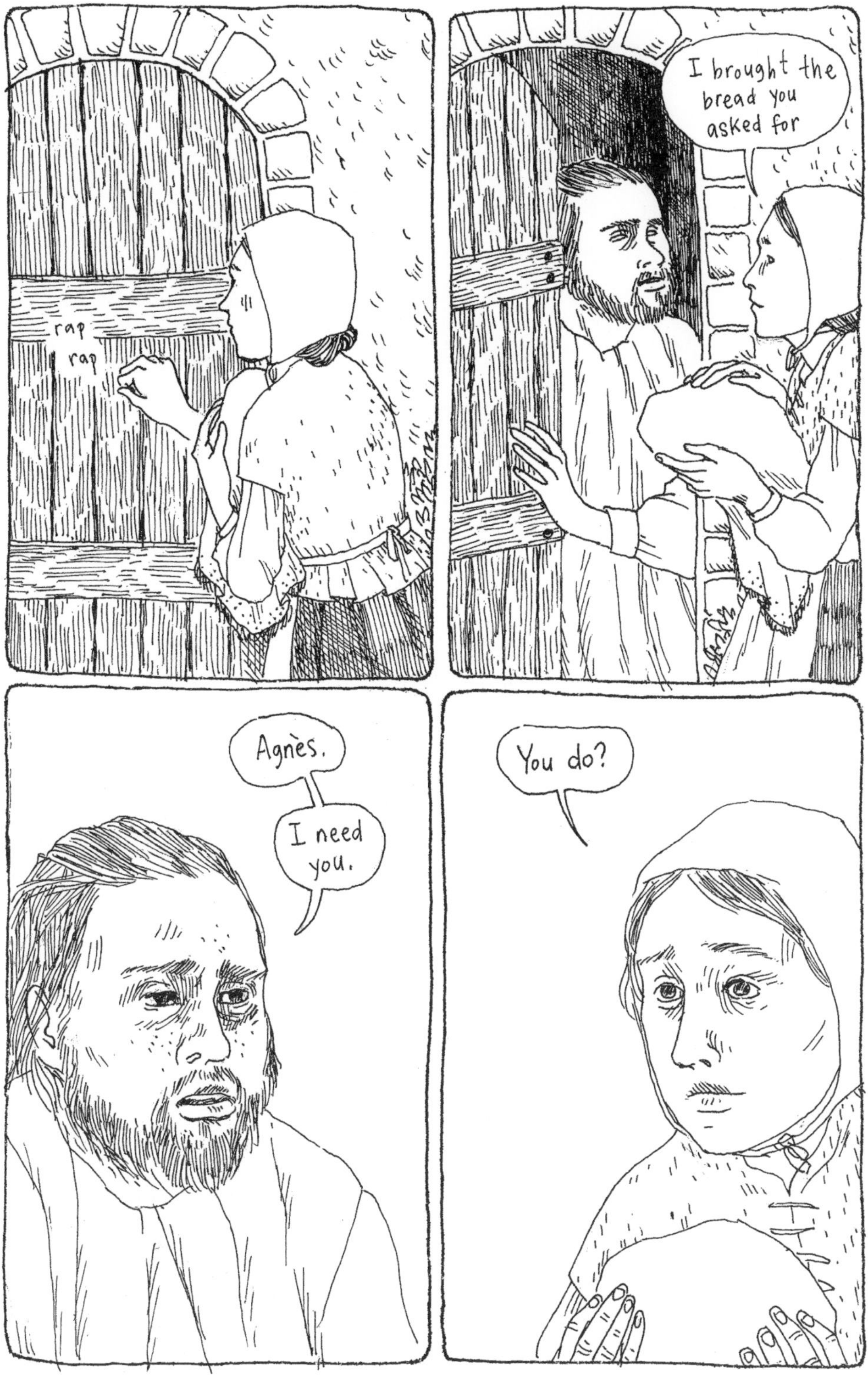
rap
rap
I brought the bread you asked for
Agnès.
I need you.
You do?

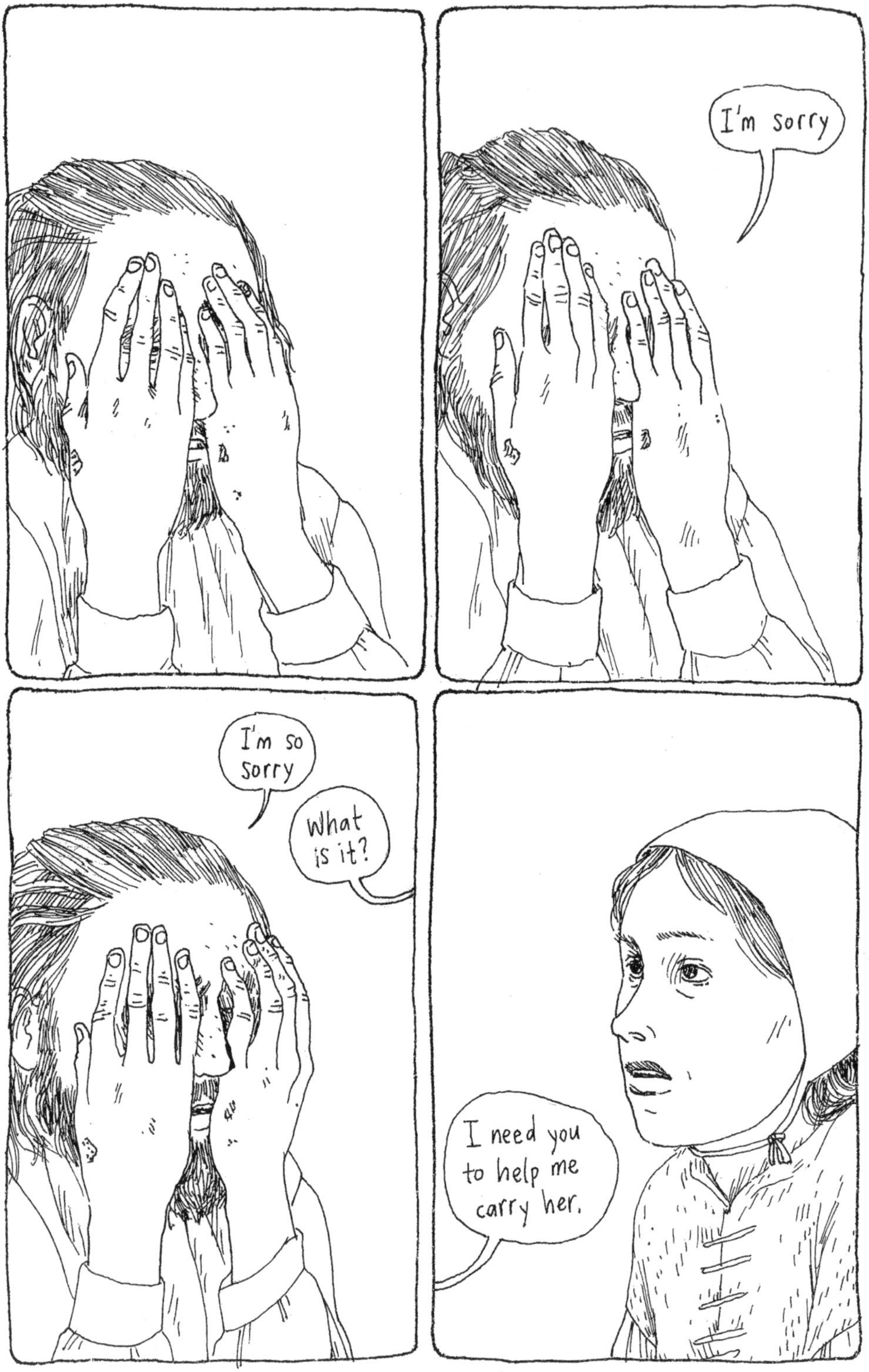
I'm sorry
I'm so sorry
What is it?
I need you to help me carry her.

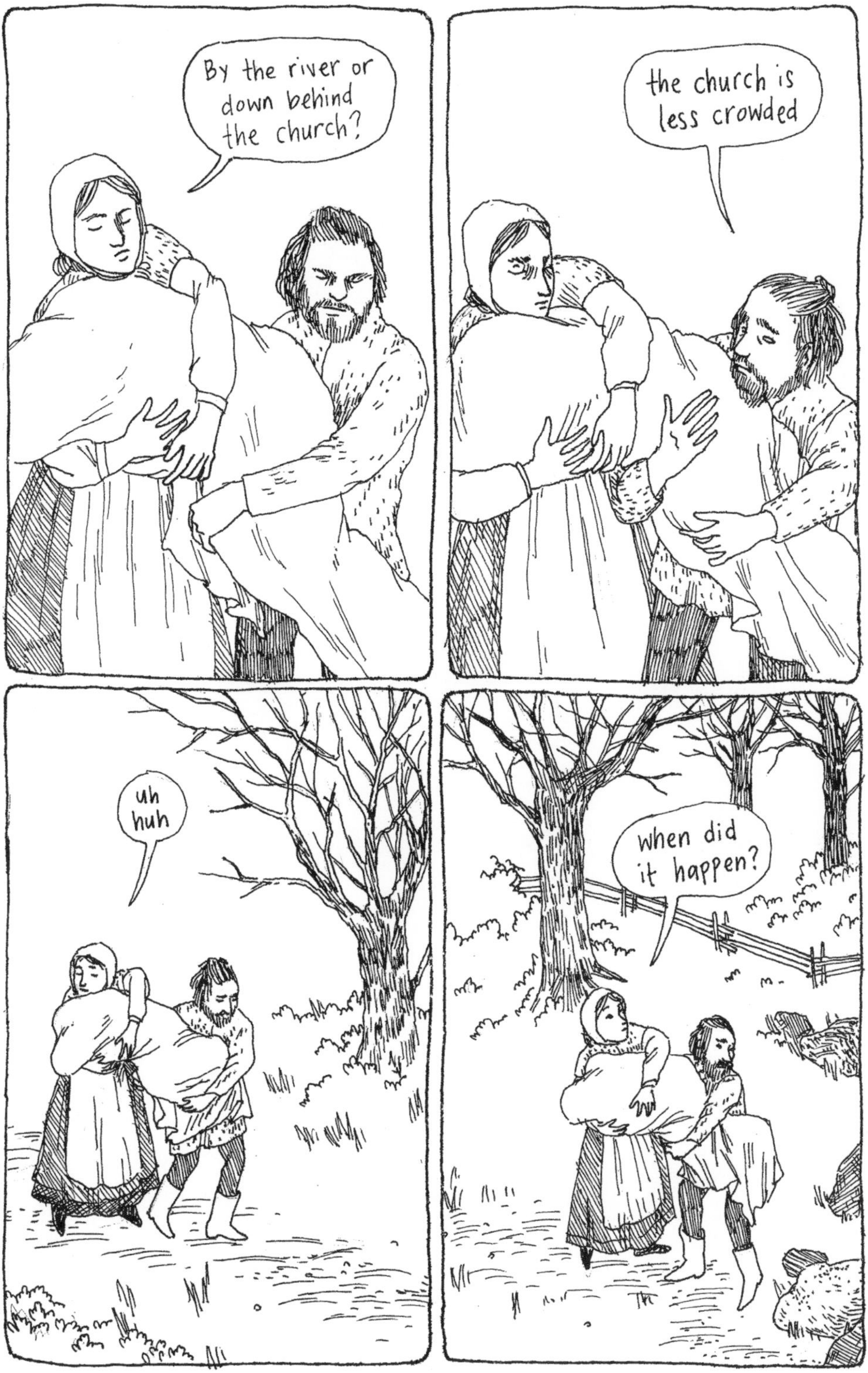
By the river or down behind the church?
the church is less crowded
uh huh
when did it happen?

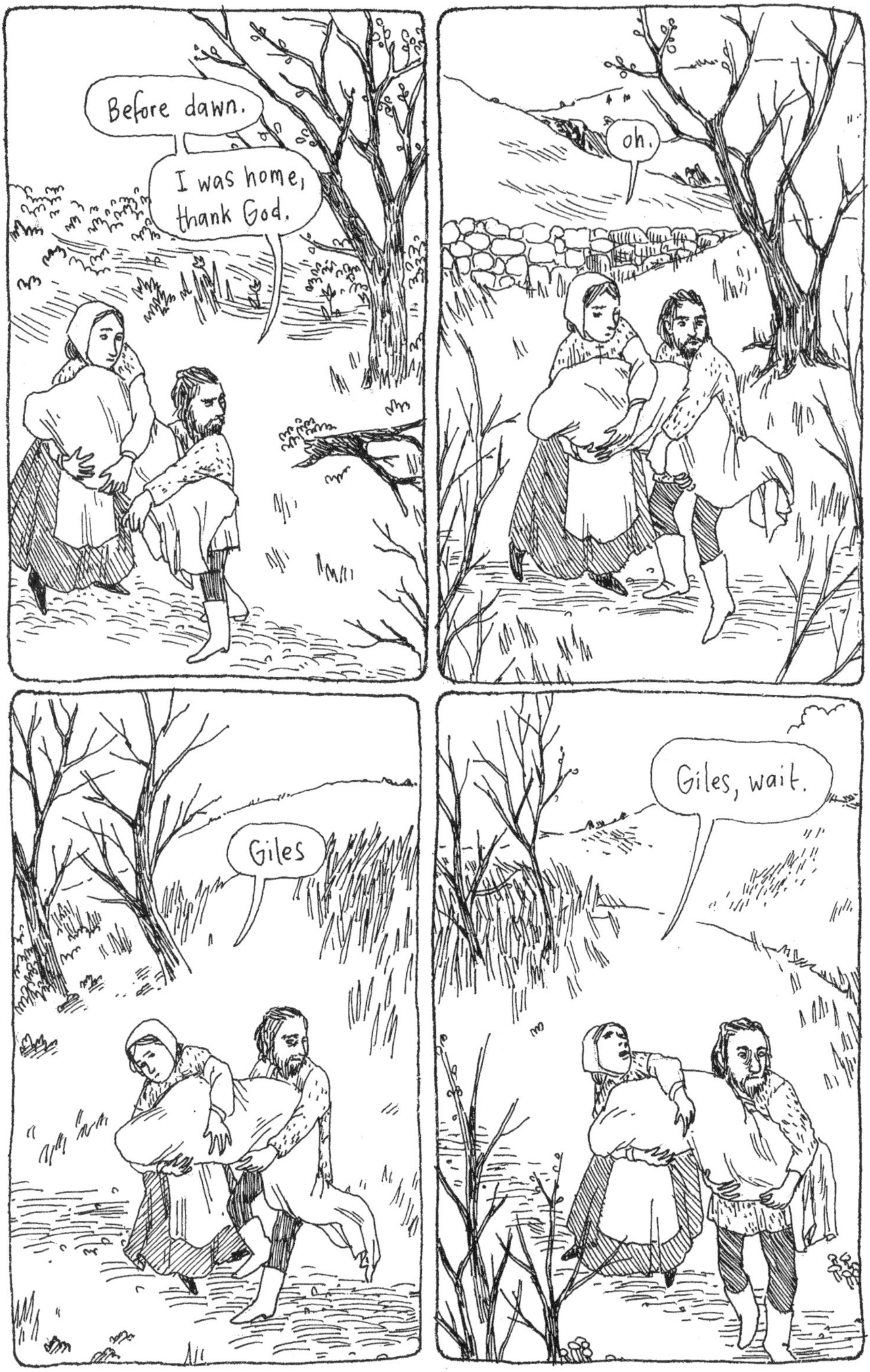
Before dawn.
I was home, thank God.
oh.
Giles
Giles, wait.

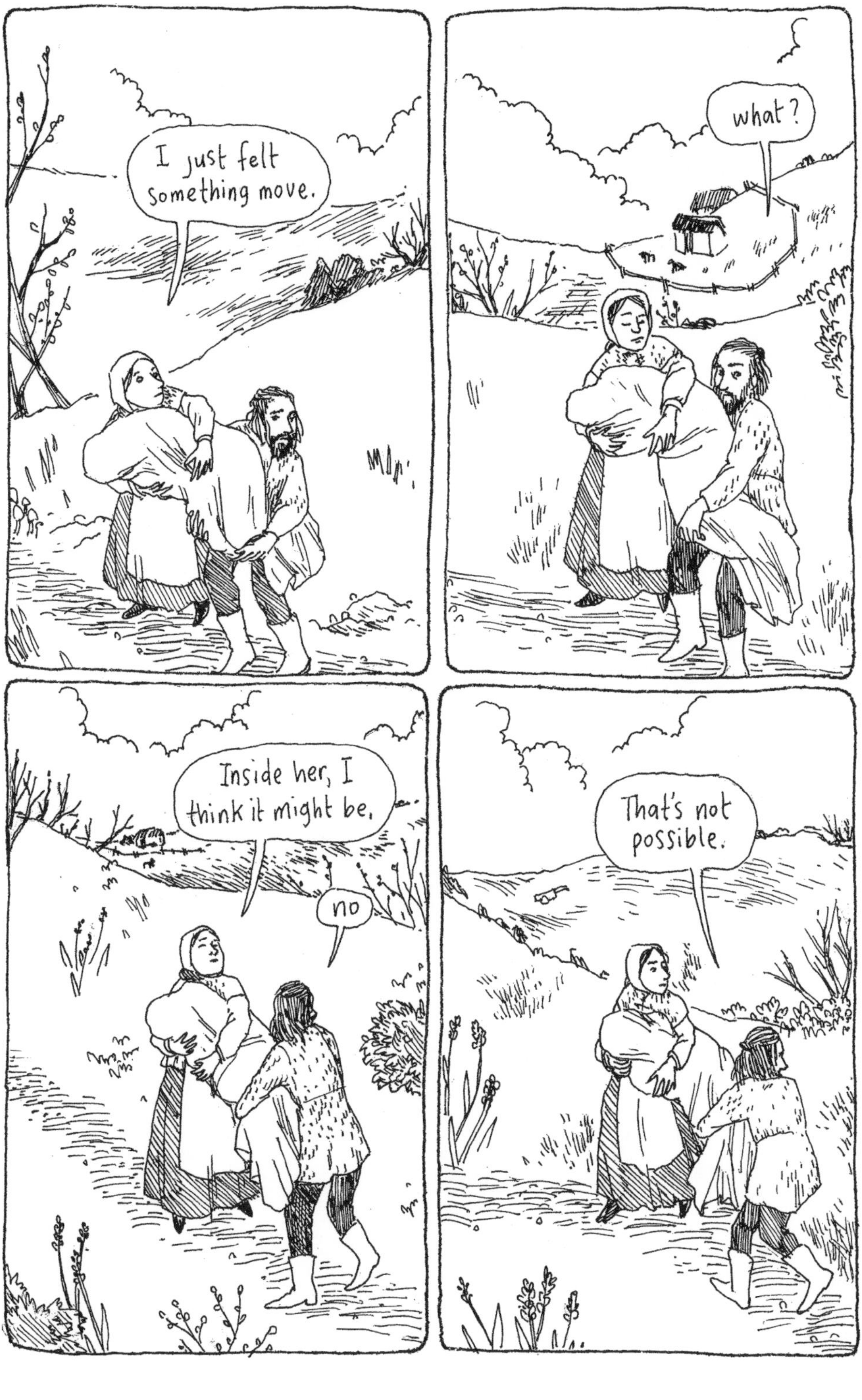
I just felt something move.
what?
Inside her, I think it might be.
no
That's not possible.

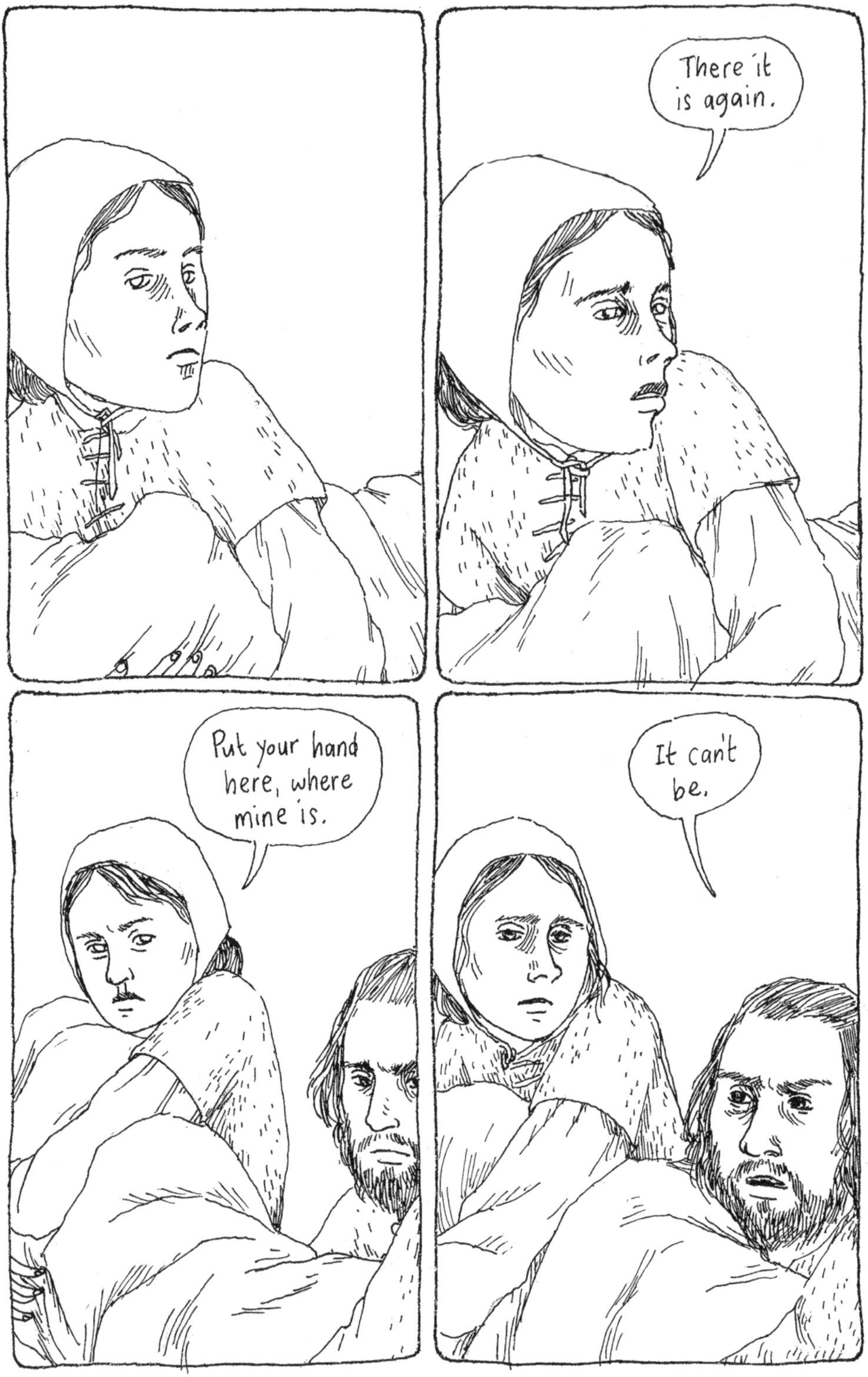
There it is again.
Put your hand here, where mine is.
It can't be.

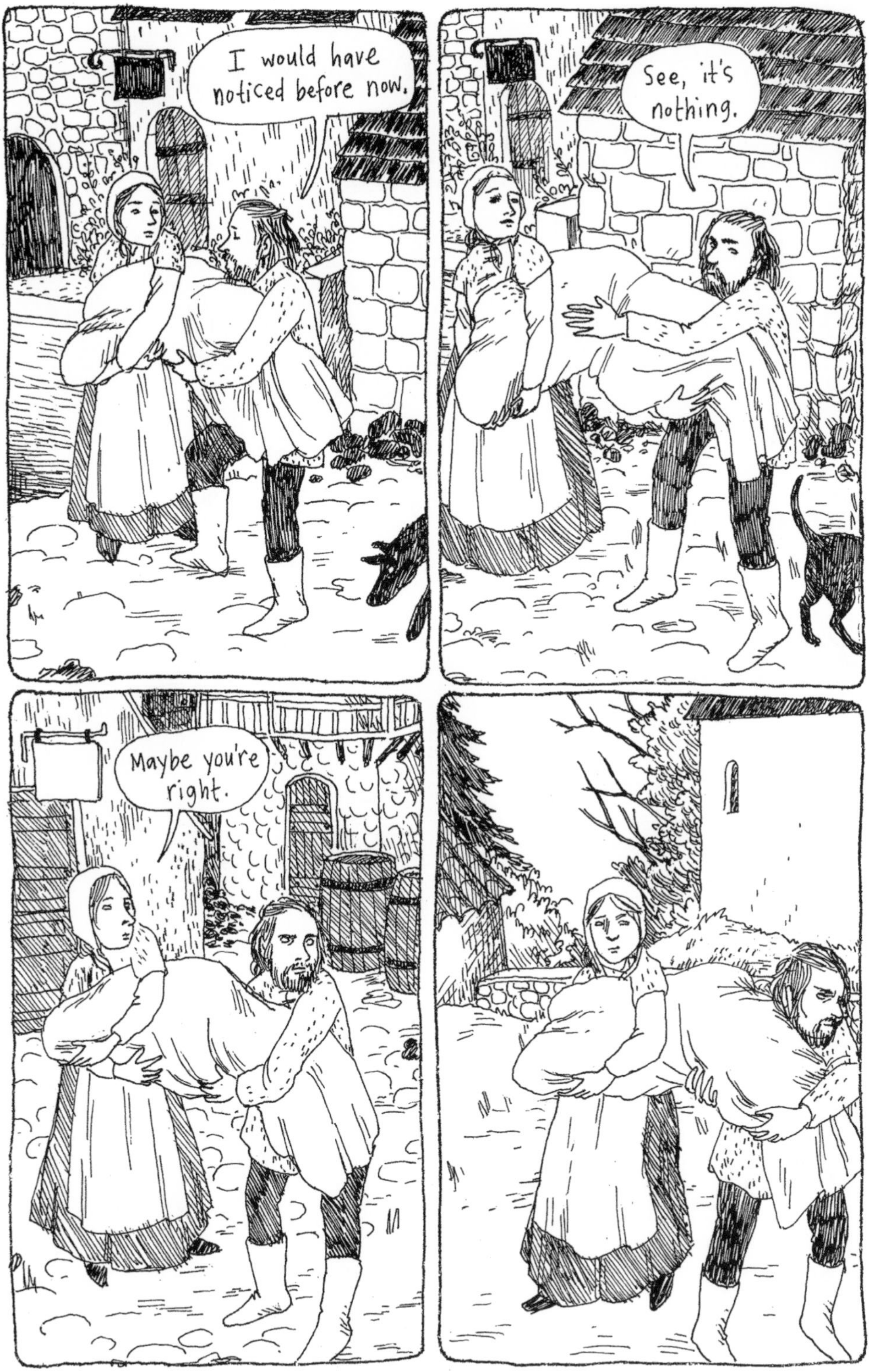
I would have noticed before now.
See, it's nothing.
Maybe you're right.

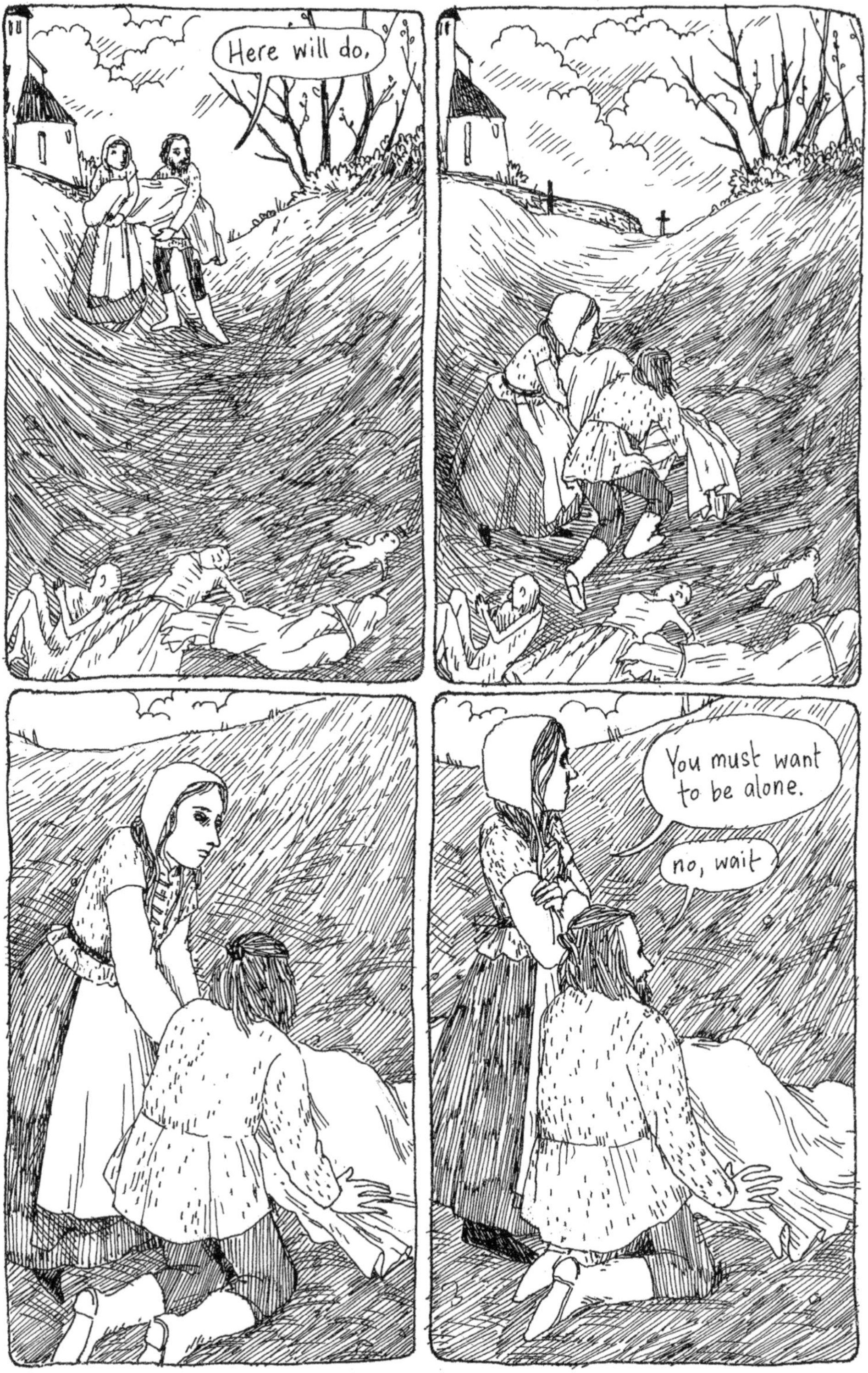
Here will do,
You must want to be alone.
no, wait

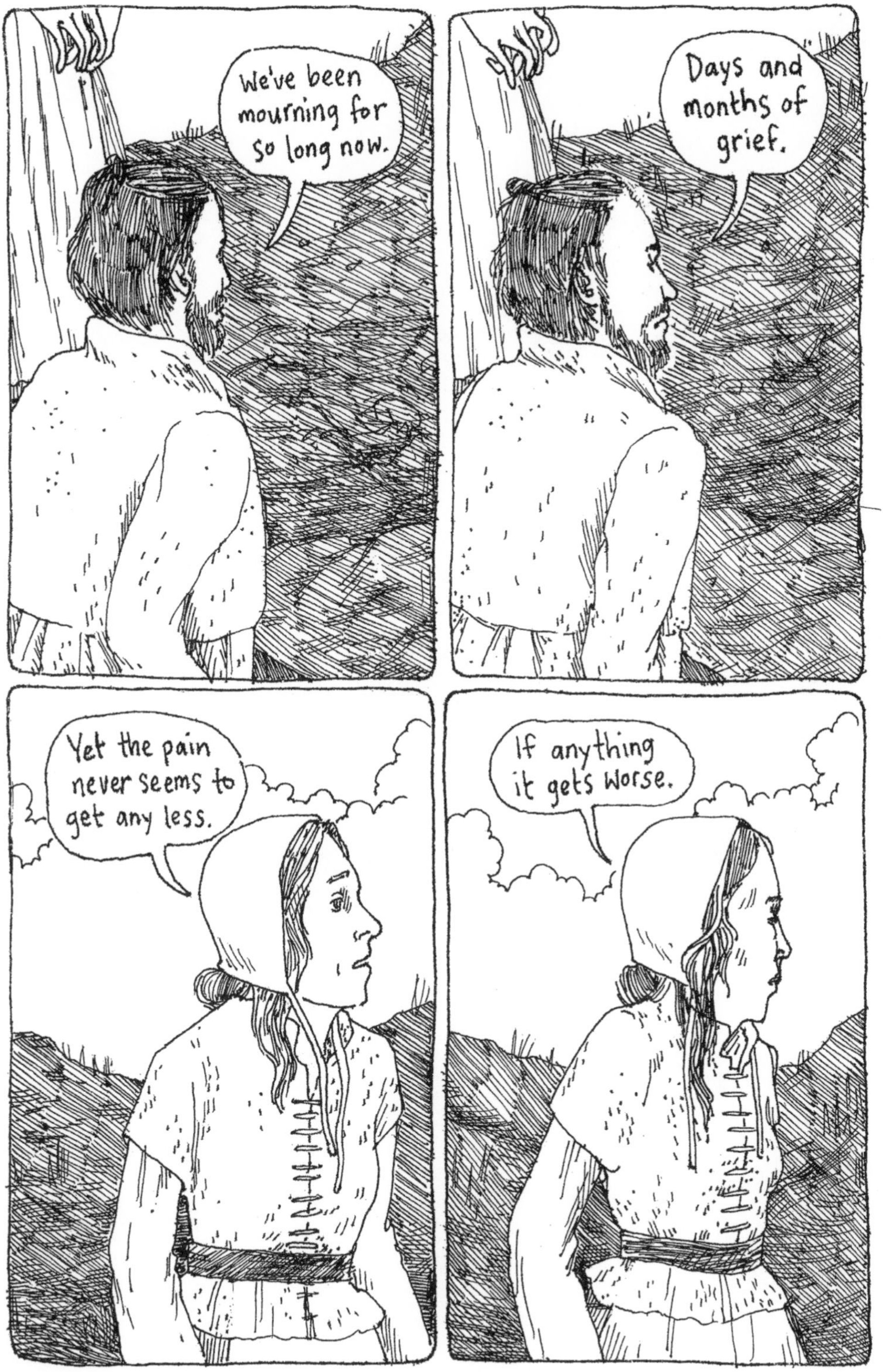
We've been mourning for so long now.
Days and months of grief.
Yet the pain never seems to get any less.
If anything it gets worse.

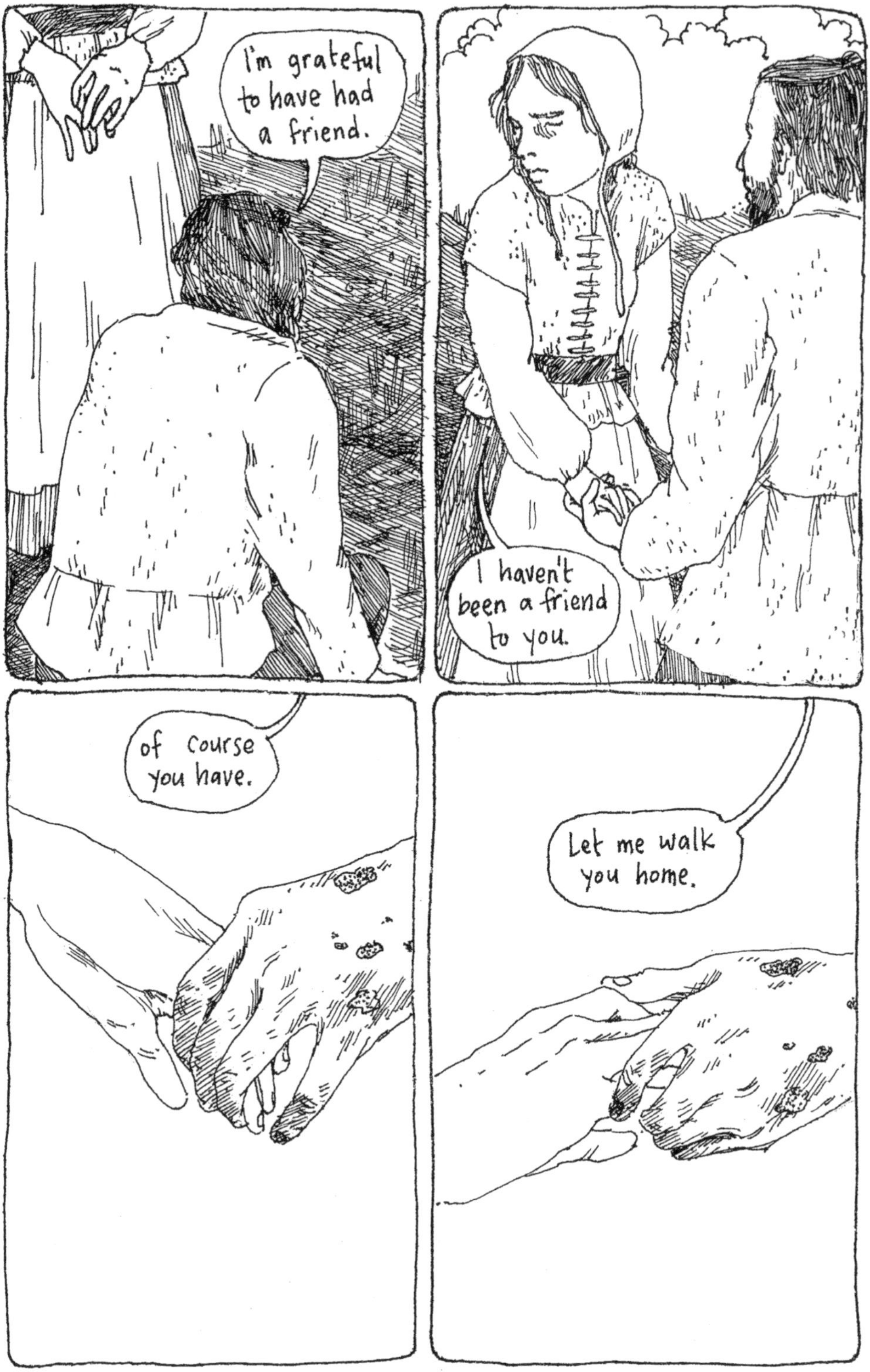
I'm grateful to have had a friend.
I haven't been a friend to you.
of course you have.
Let me walk you home.

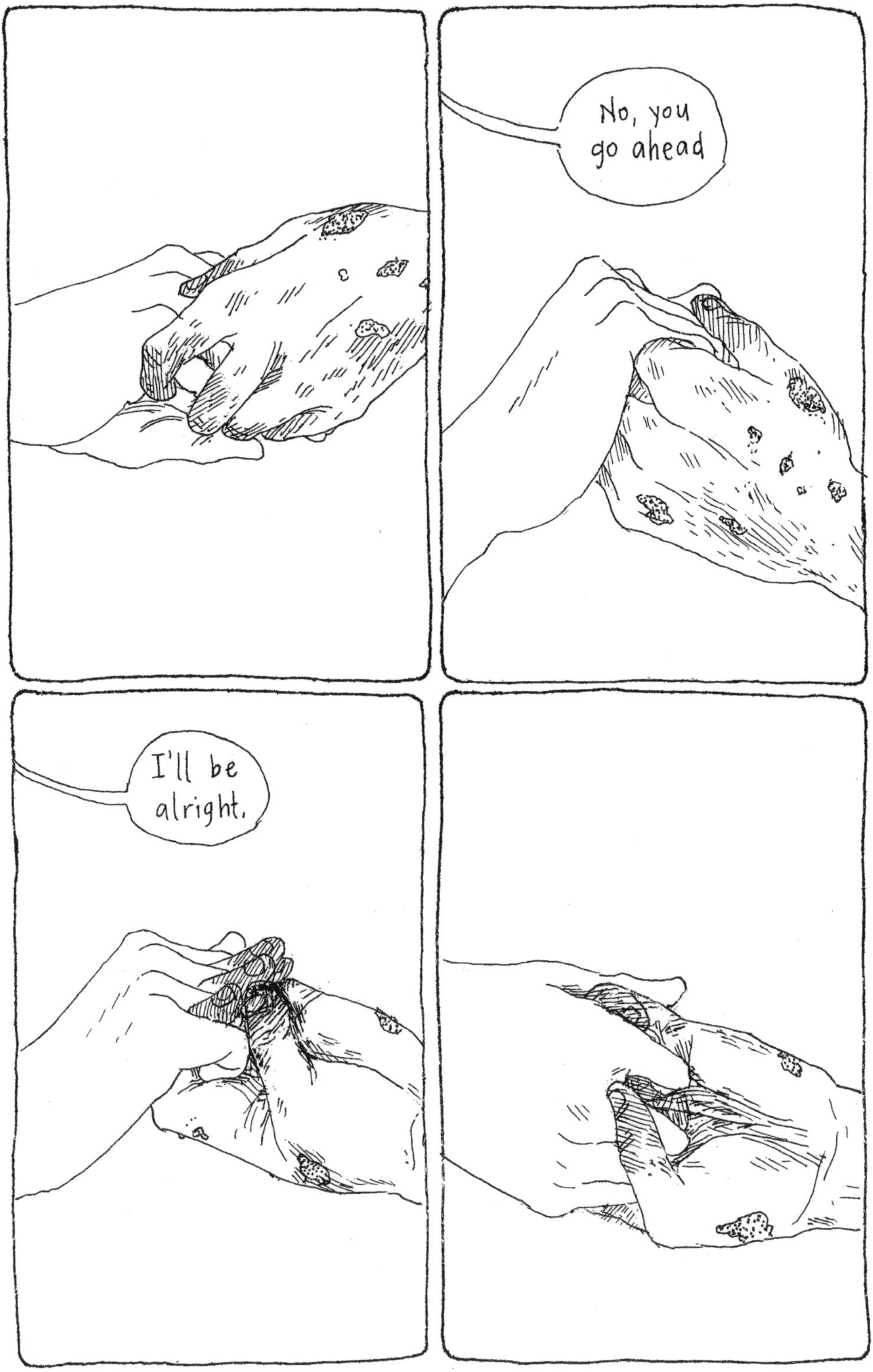
No, you go ahead
I'll be alright.

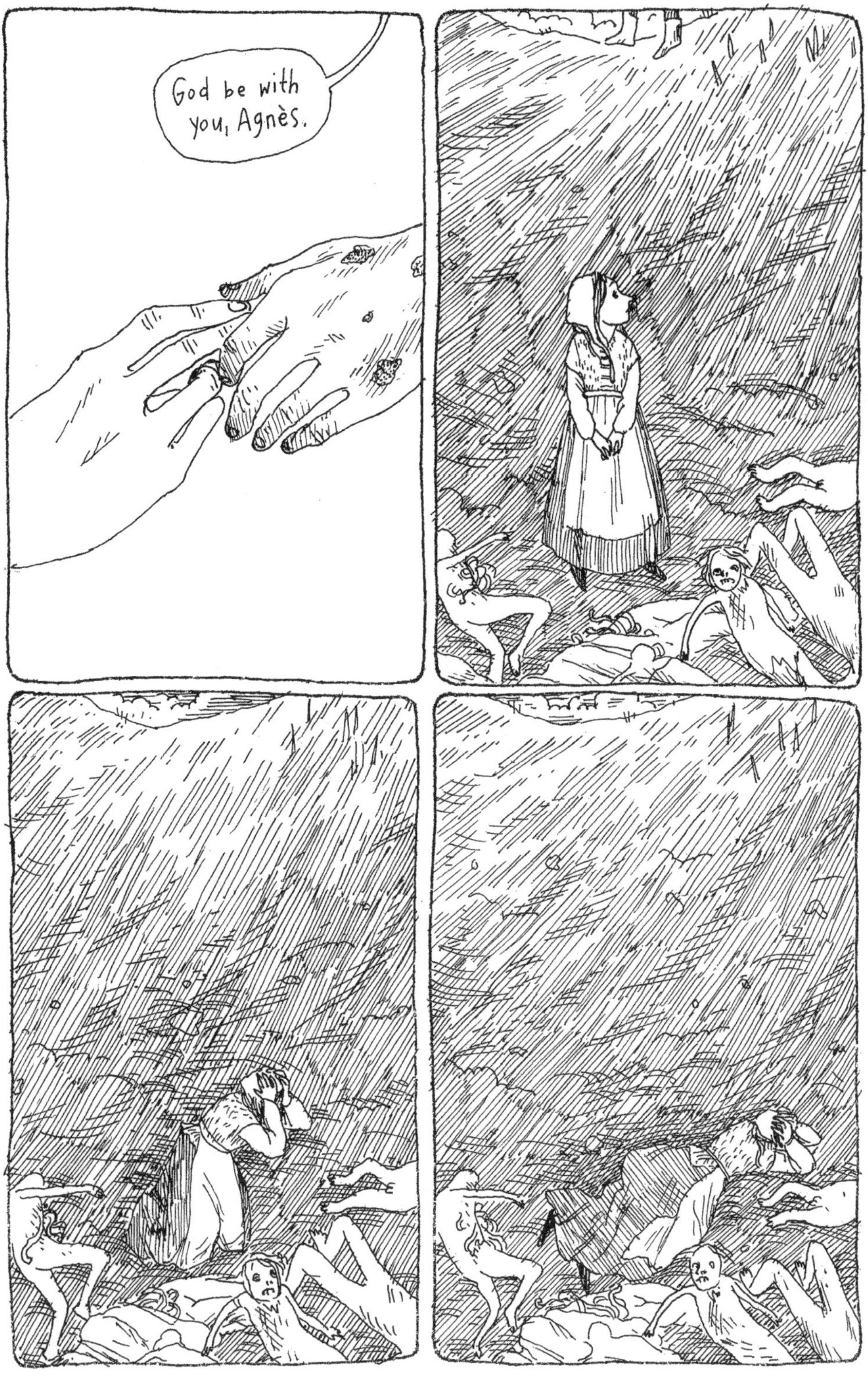
God be with you, Agnès.

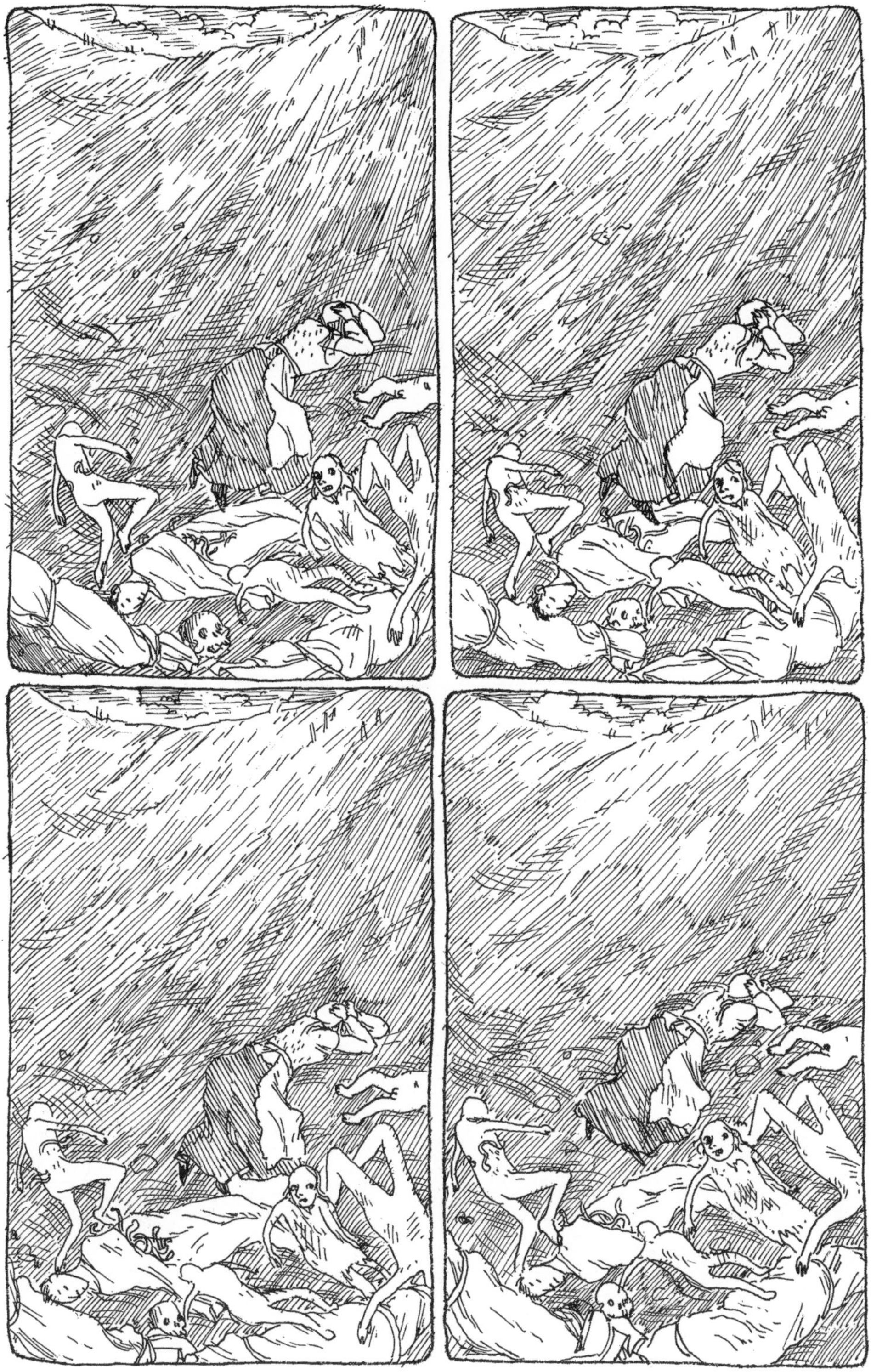

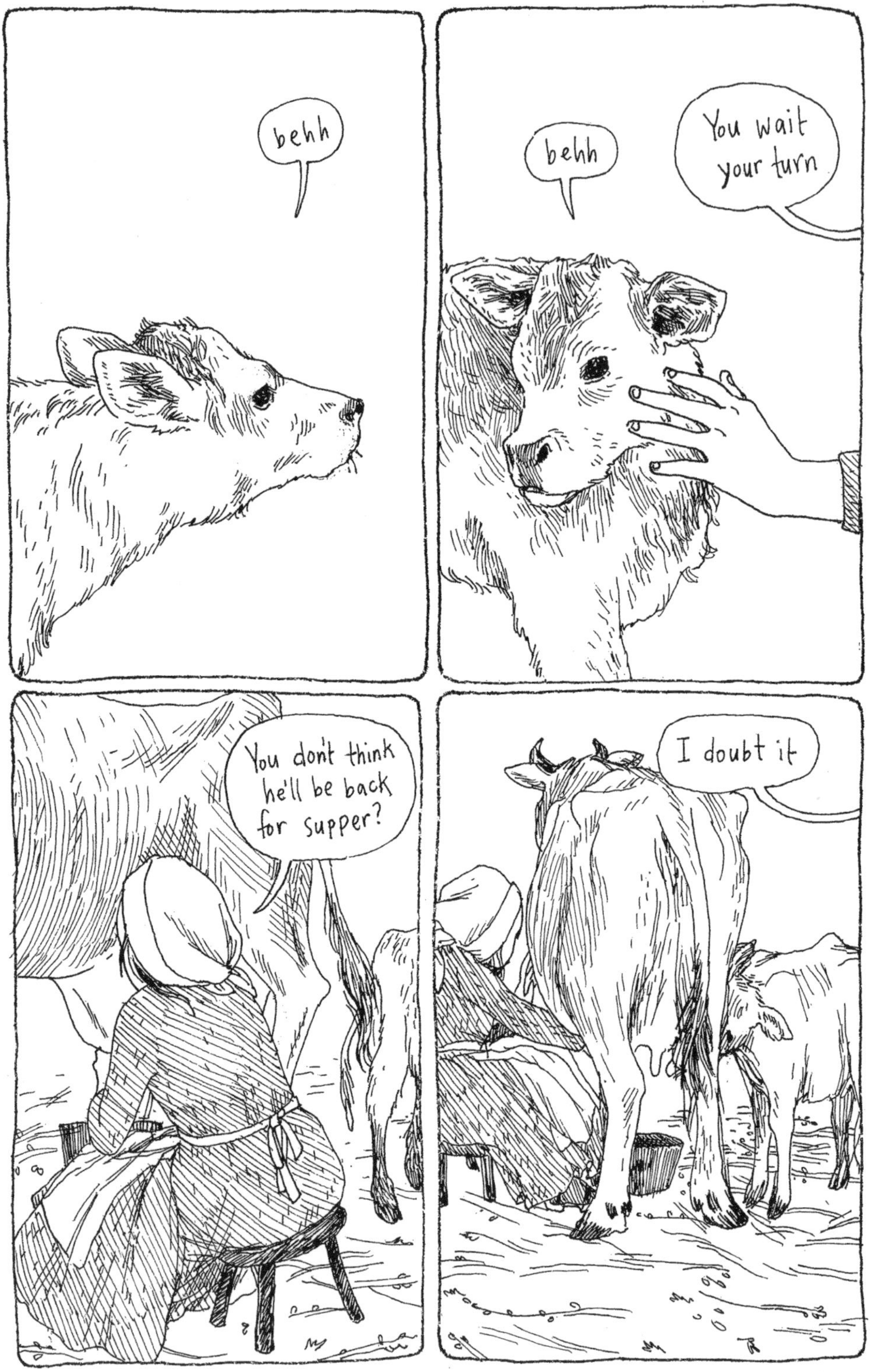
behh
behh
You wait your turn
You don't think he'll be back for supper?
I doubt it

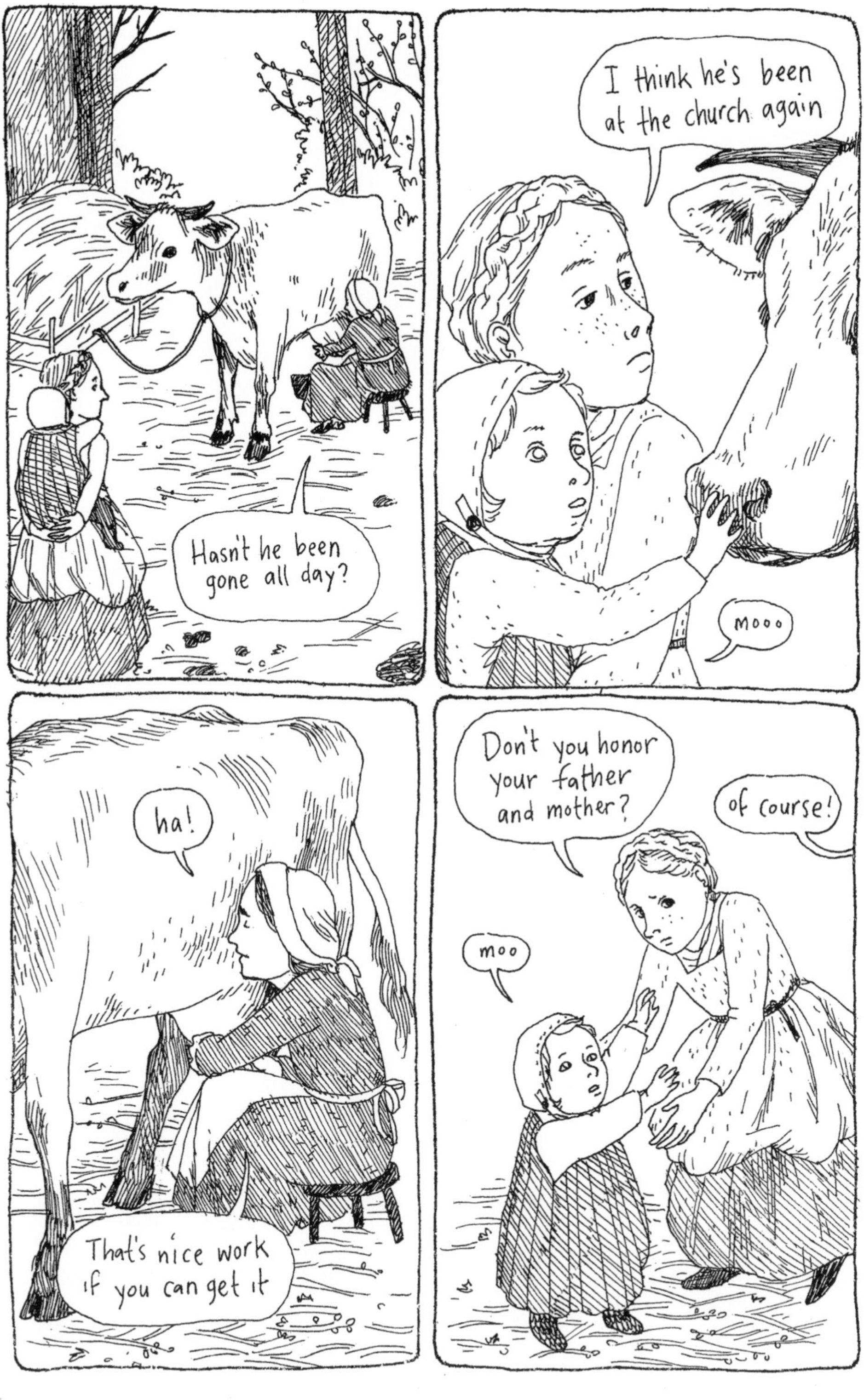
Hasn't he been gone all day?
I think he's been at the church again
mooo
ha!
That's nice work if you can get it
Don't you honor your father and mother?
of course!
moo

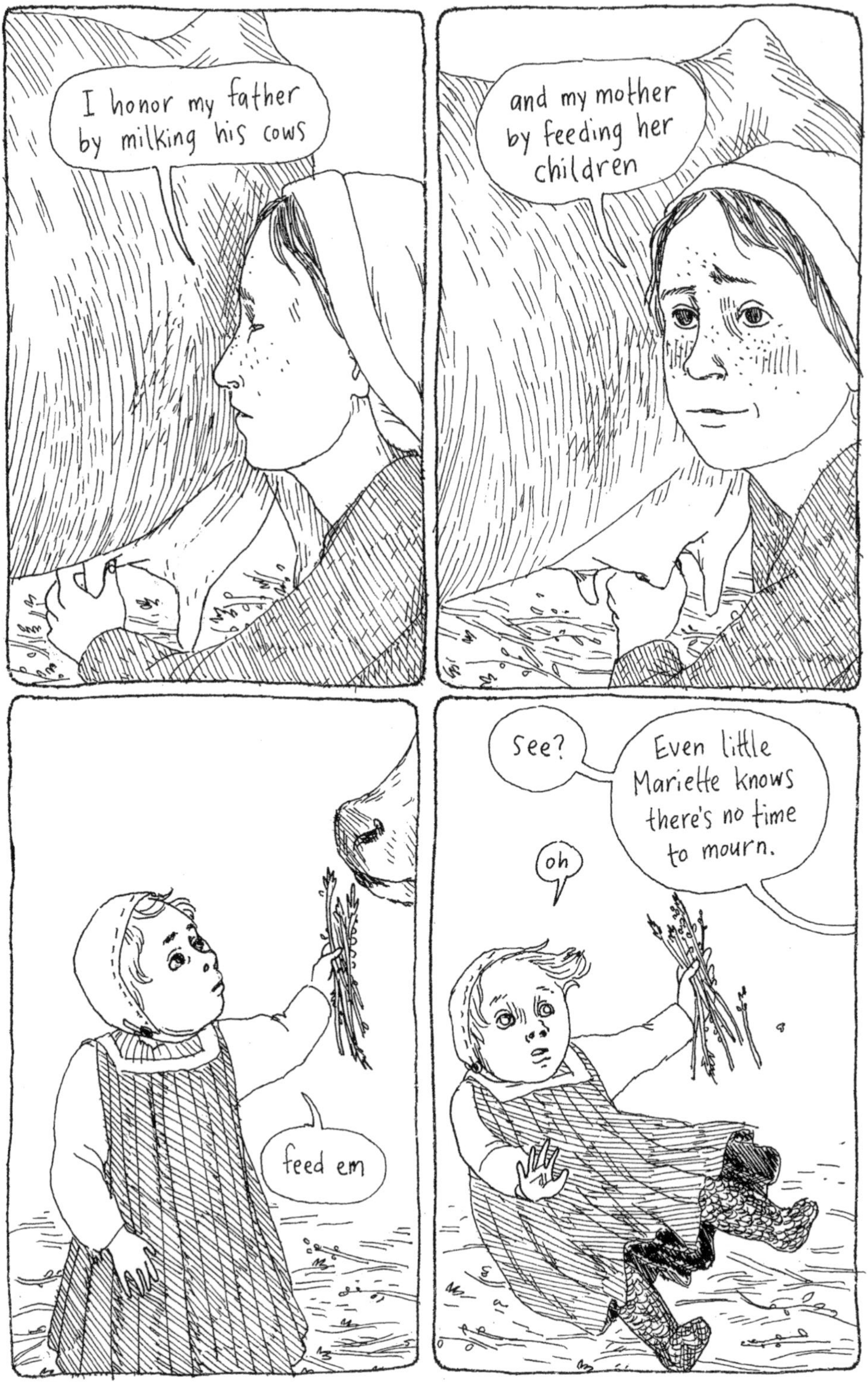
I honor my father by milking his cows
and my mother by feeding her children
feed em
See?
Even little Mariette knows there's no time to mourn.
oh

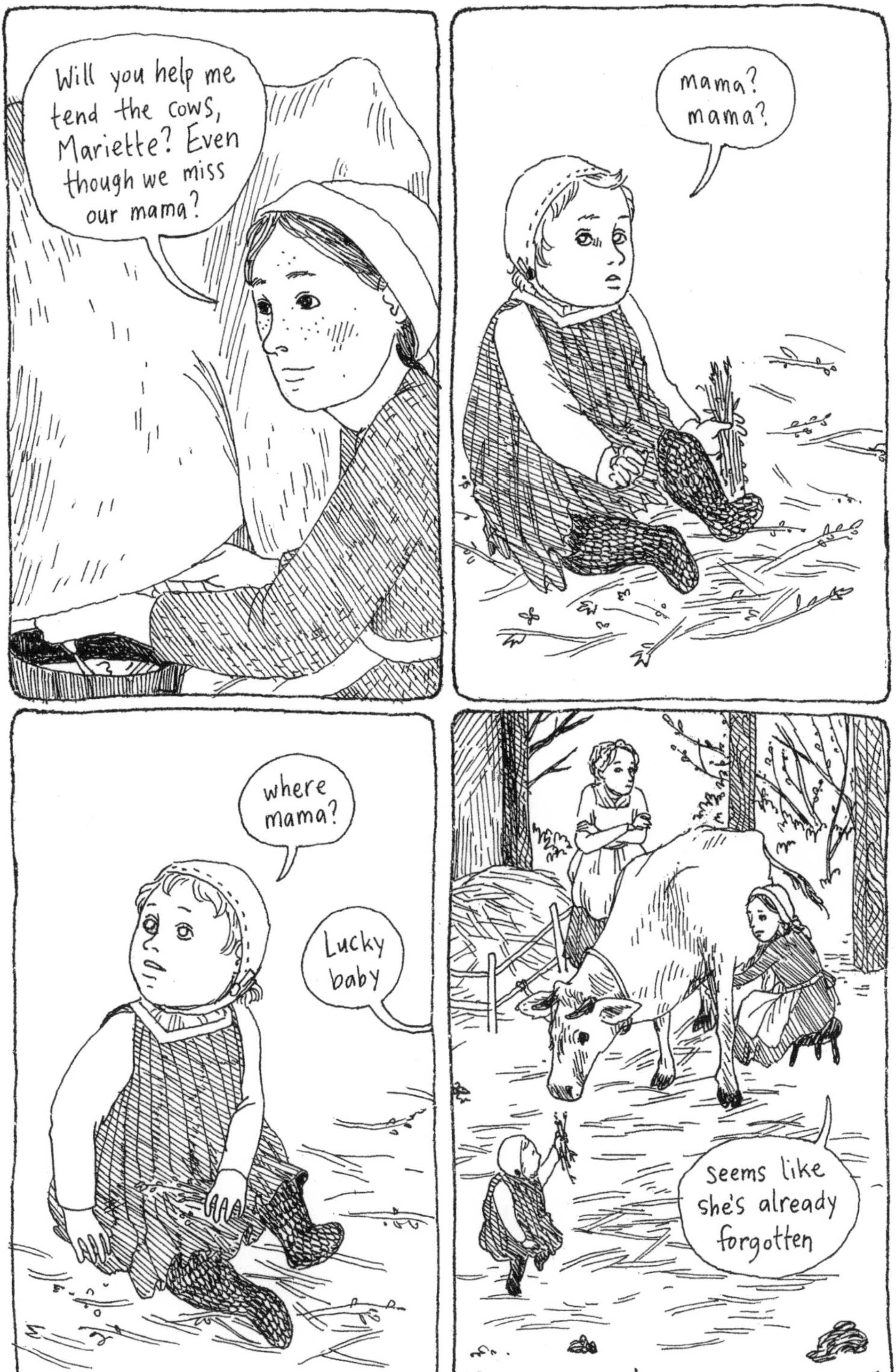
Will you help me tend the cows, Mariette? Even though we miss our mama?
mama? mama?
where mama?
Lucky baby
seems like she's already forgotten

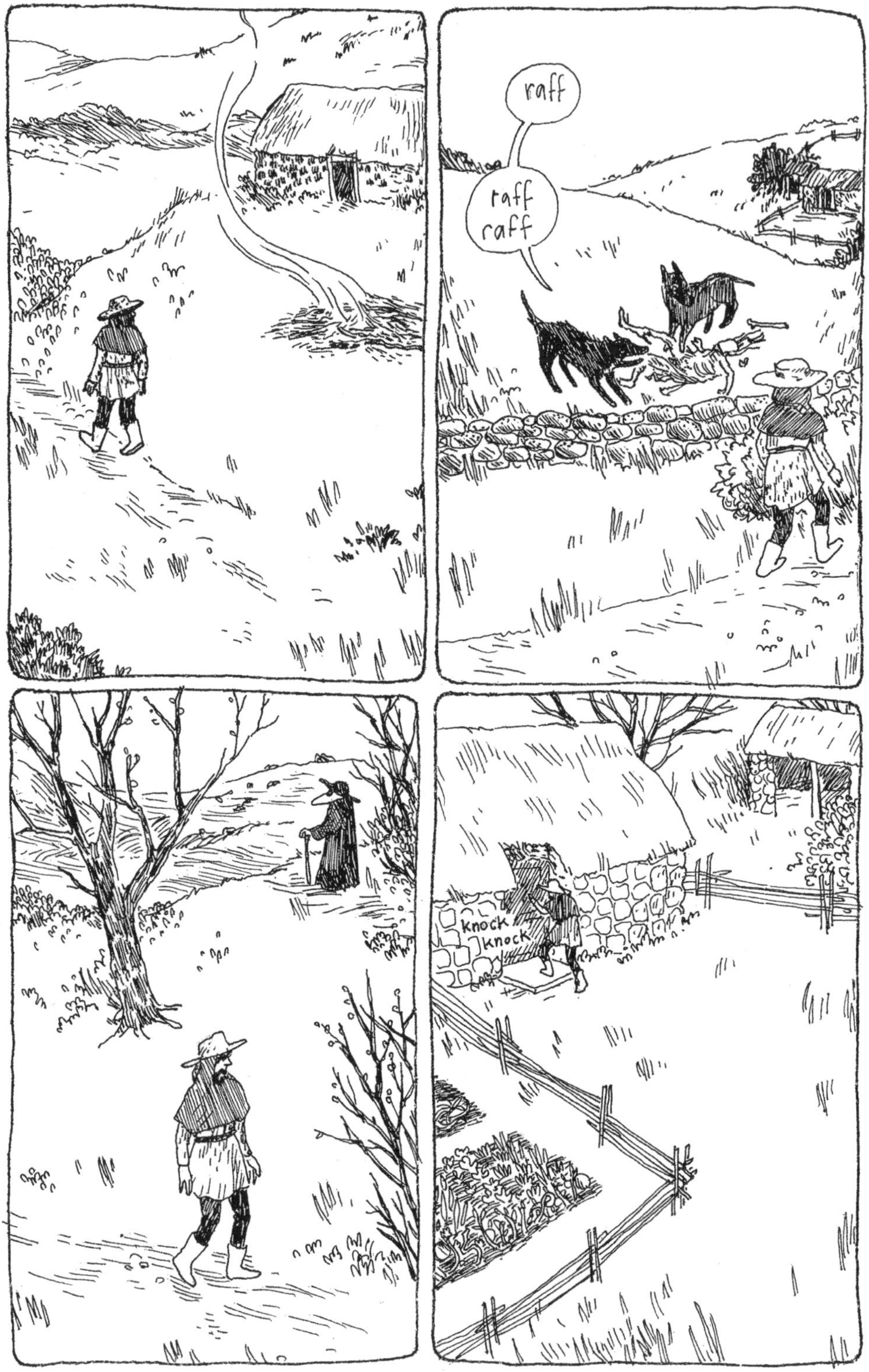
raff
raff
raff
knock
knock

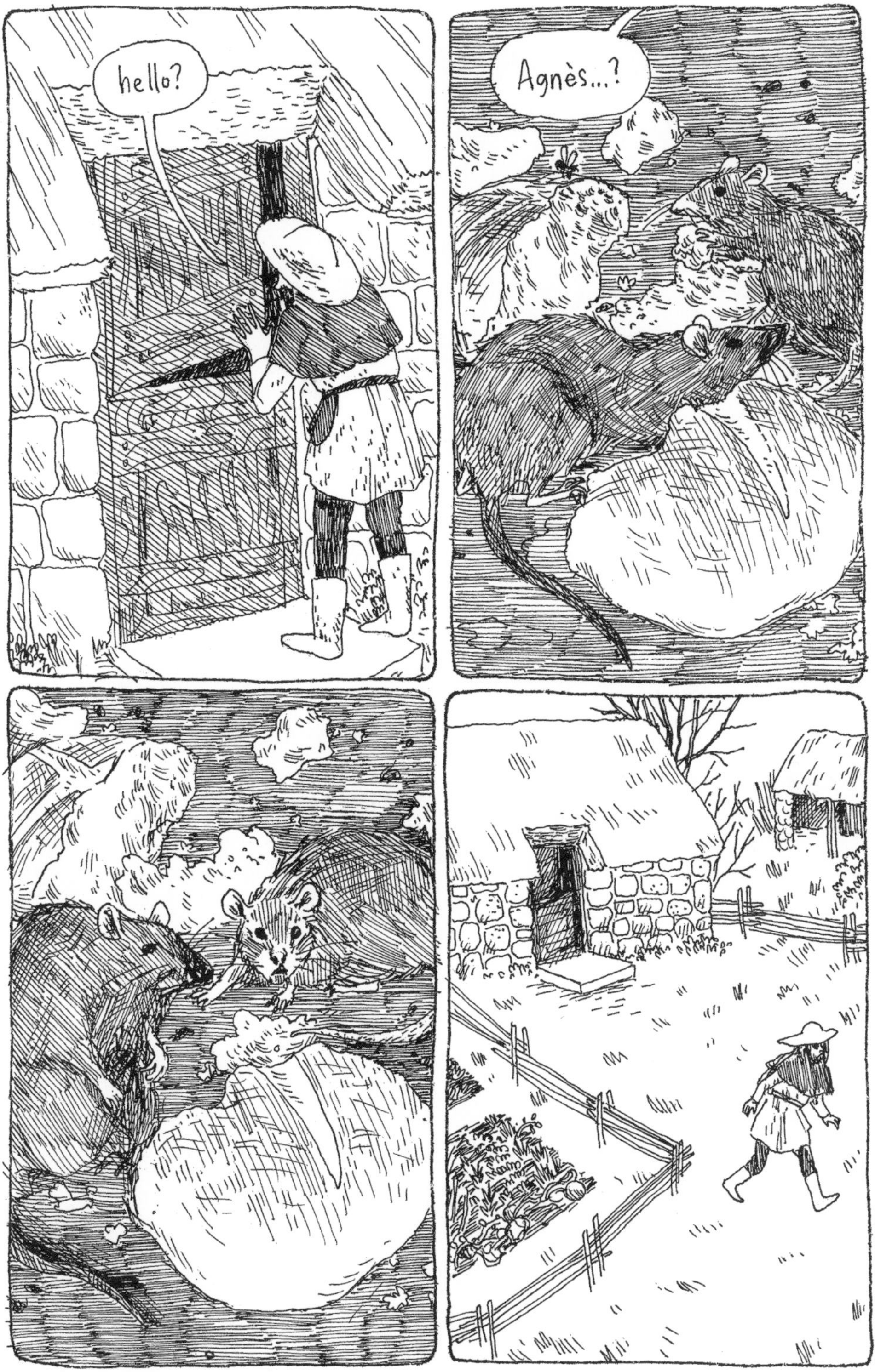
hello?
Agnès...?

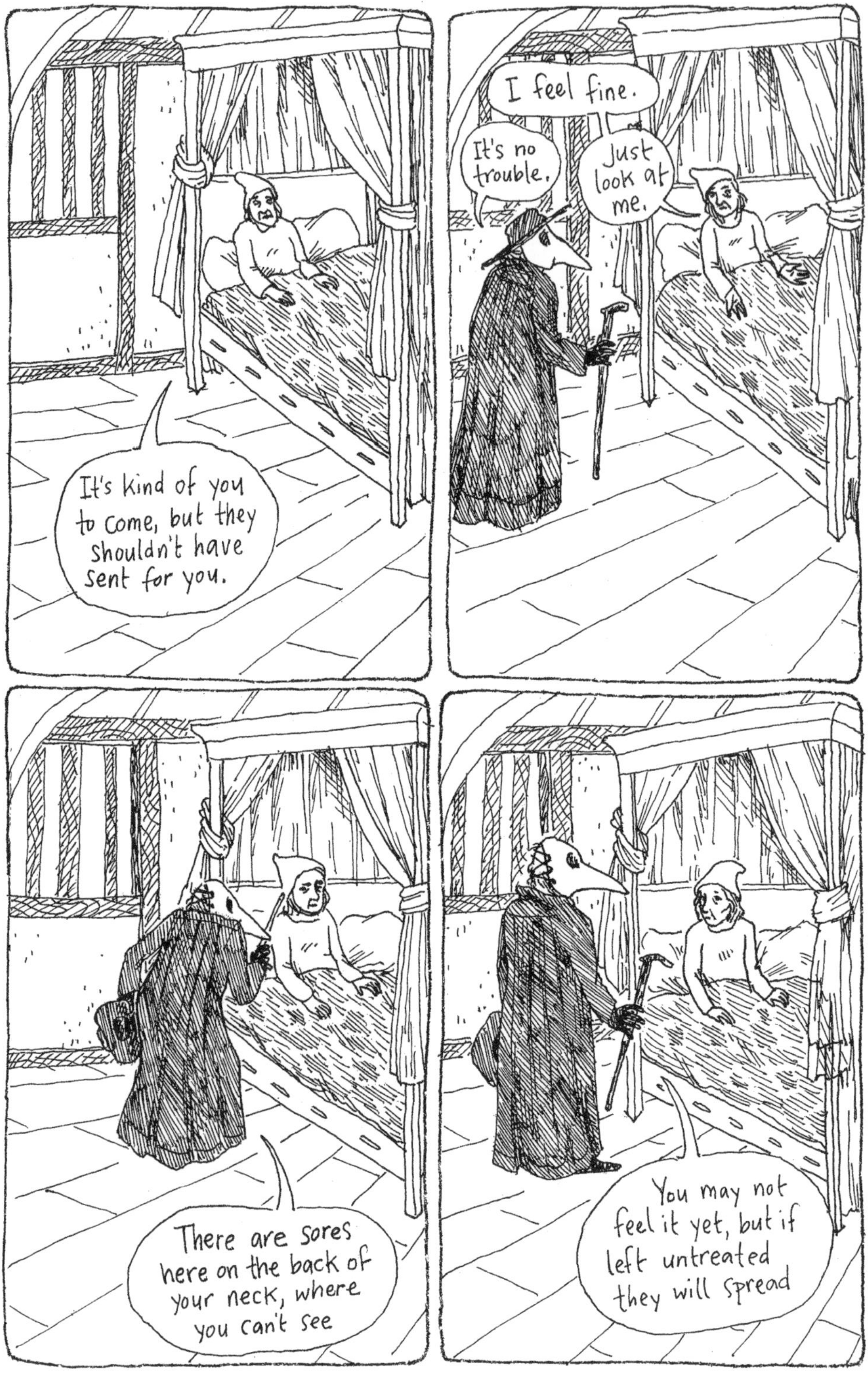
It's kind of you to come, but they shouldn't have sent for you.
I feel fine.
It's no trouble.
Just look at me.
There are sores here on the back of your neck, where you can't see
You may not feel it yet, but if left untreated they will spread

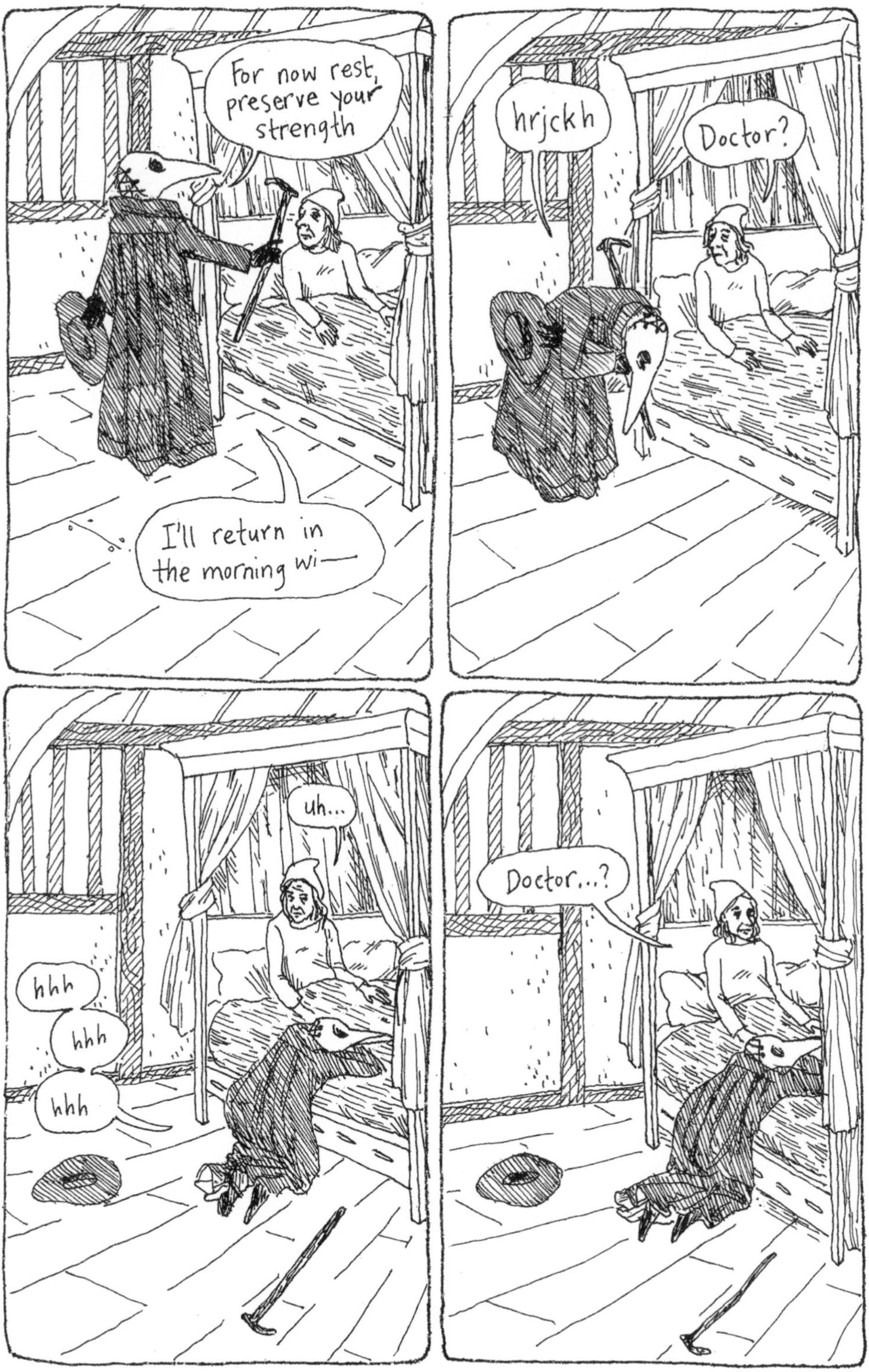

For now rest, preserve your strength
I'll return in the morning wi—
hrjckh
Doctor?
uh...
hhh
hhh
hhh
Doctor...?

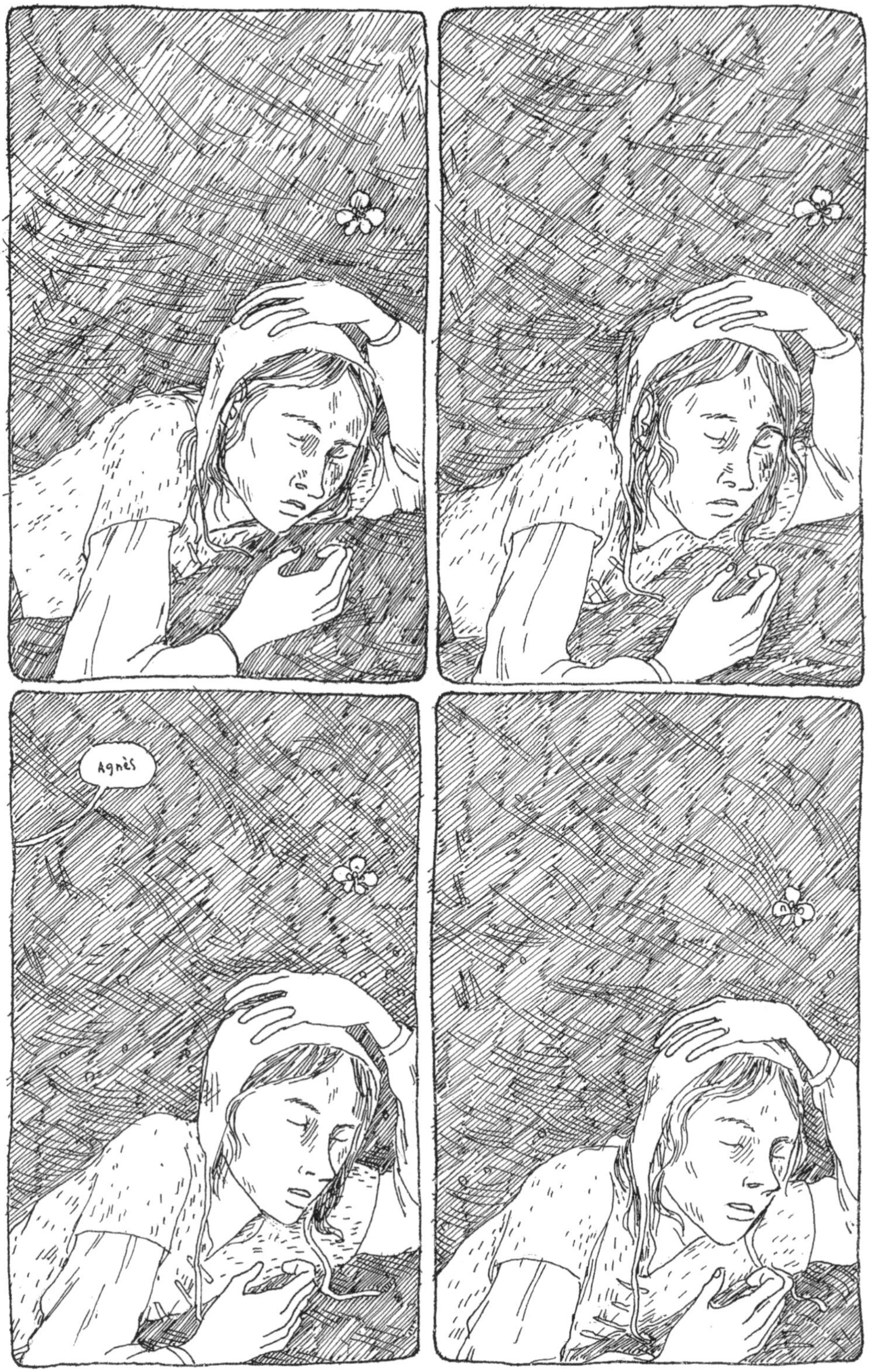
Agnès

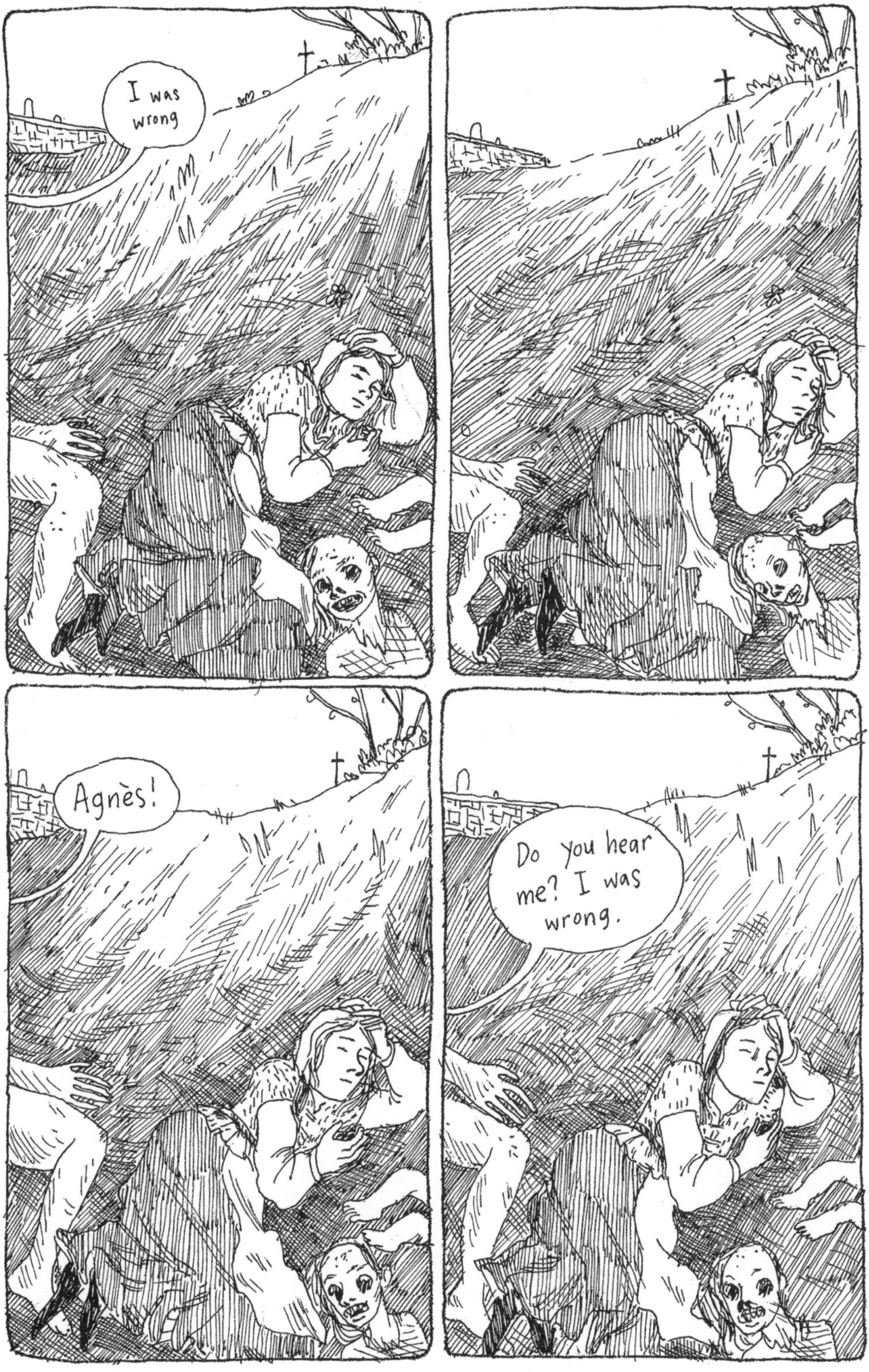
I was wrong
Agnès!
Do you hear me? I was wrong.

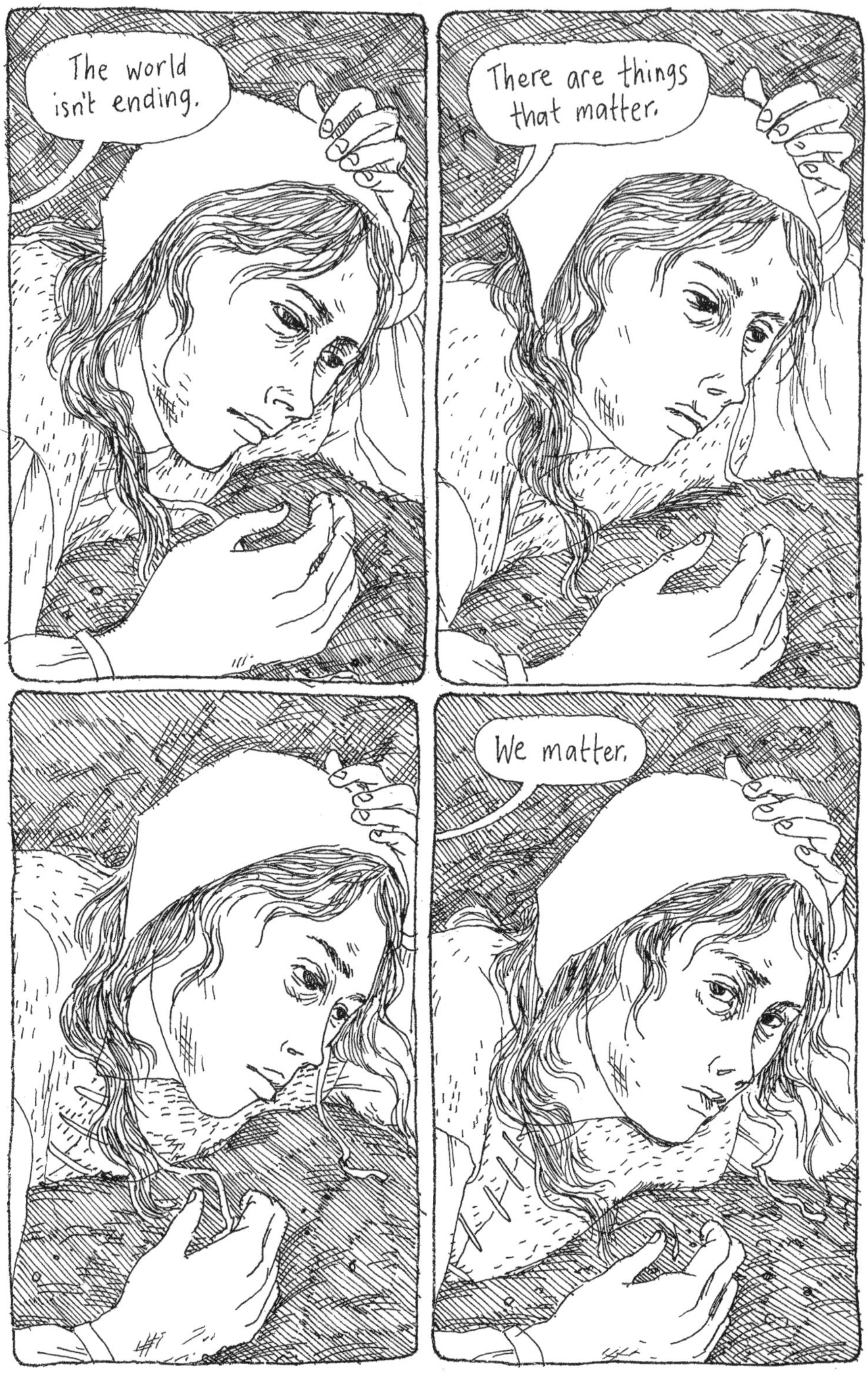
The world isn't ending.
There are things that matter.
We matter.

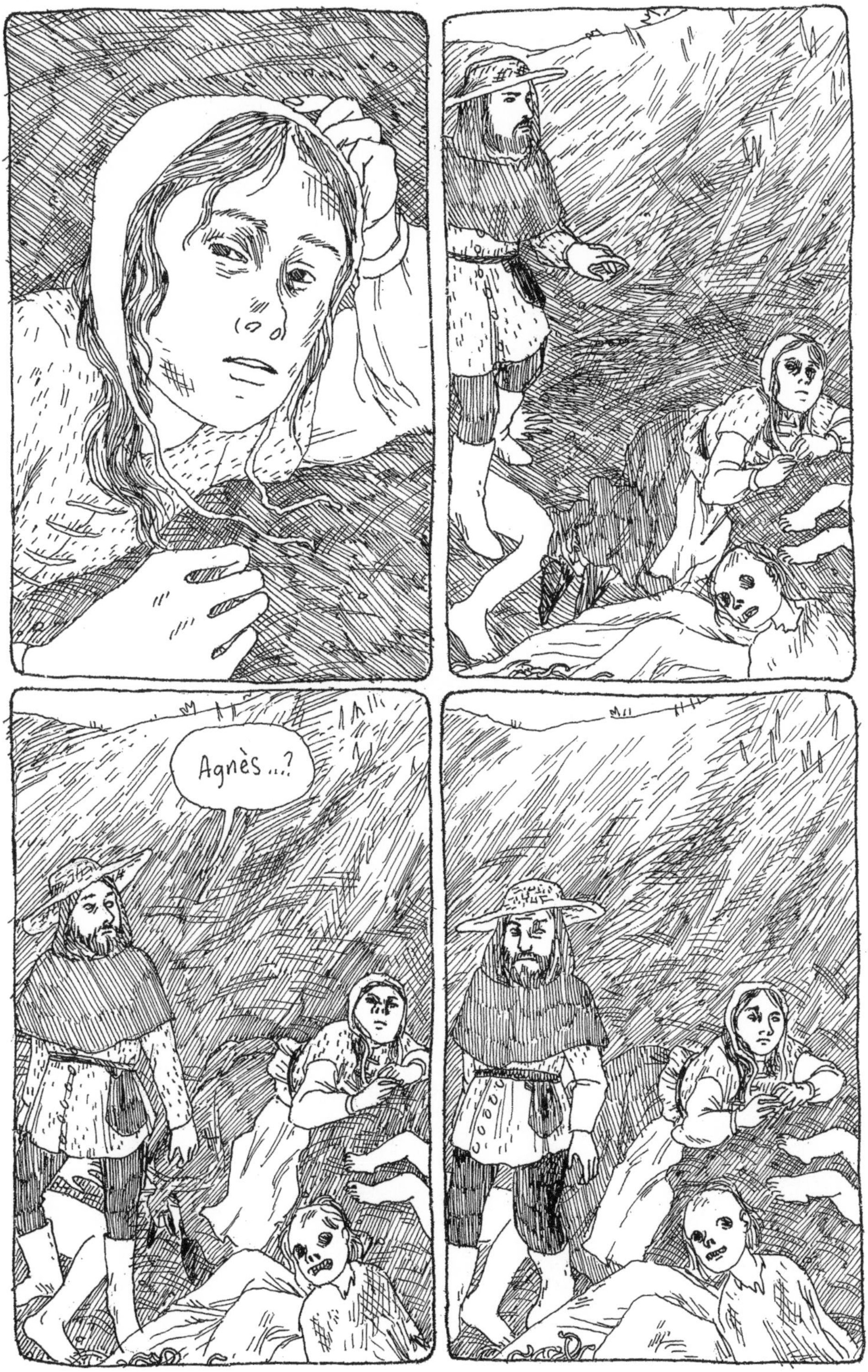
Agnès...?

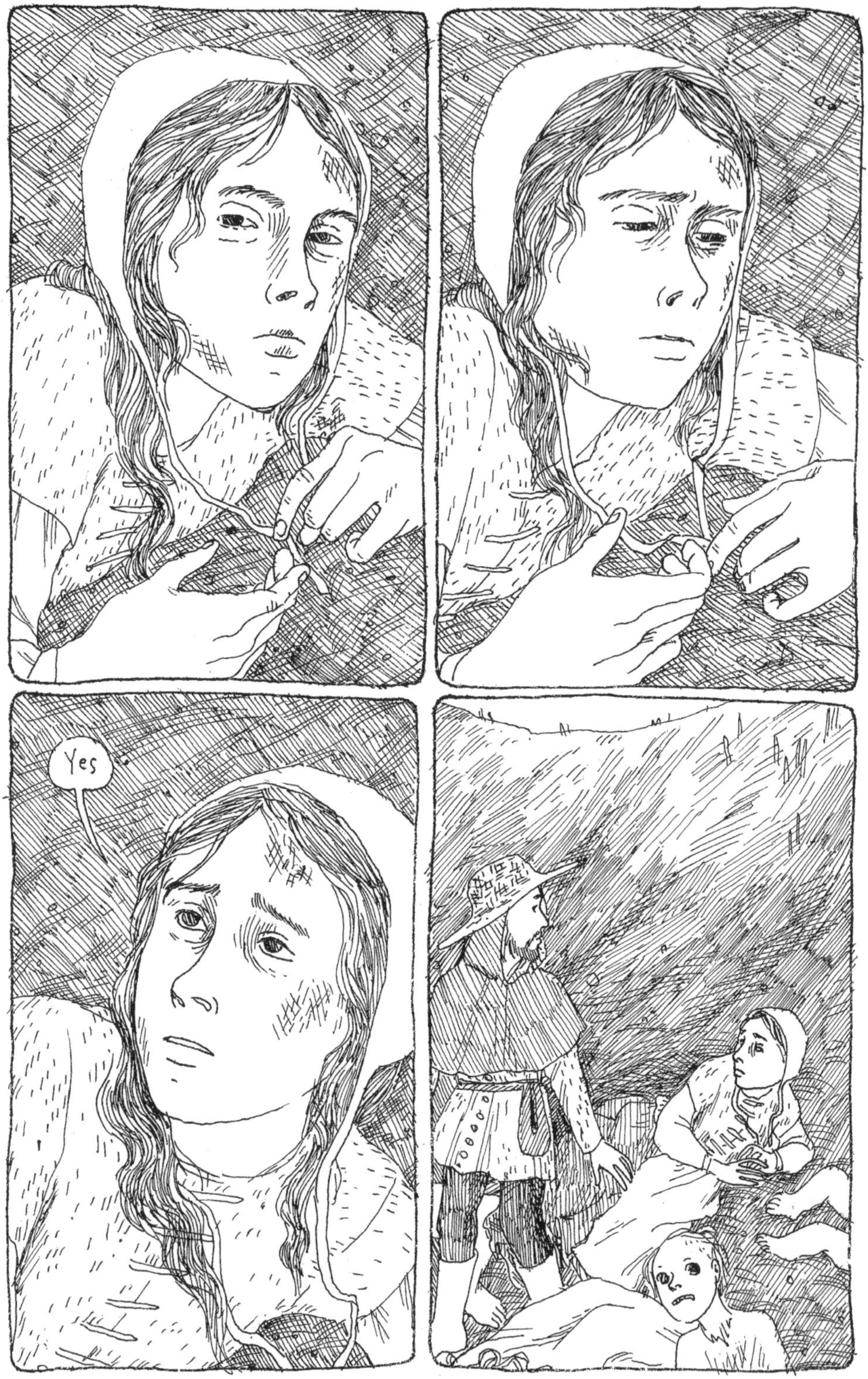
Yes

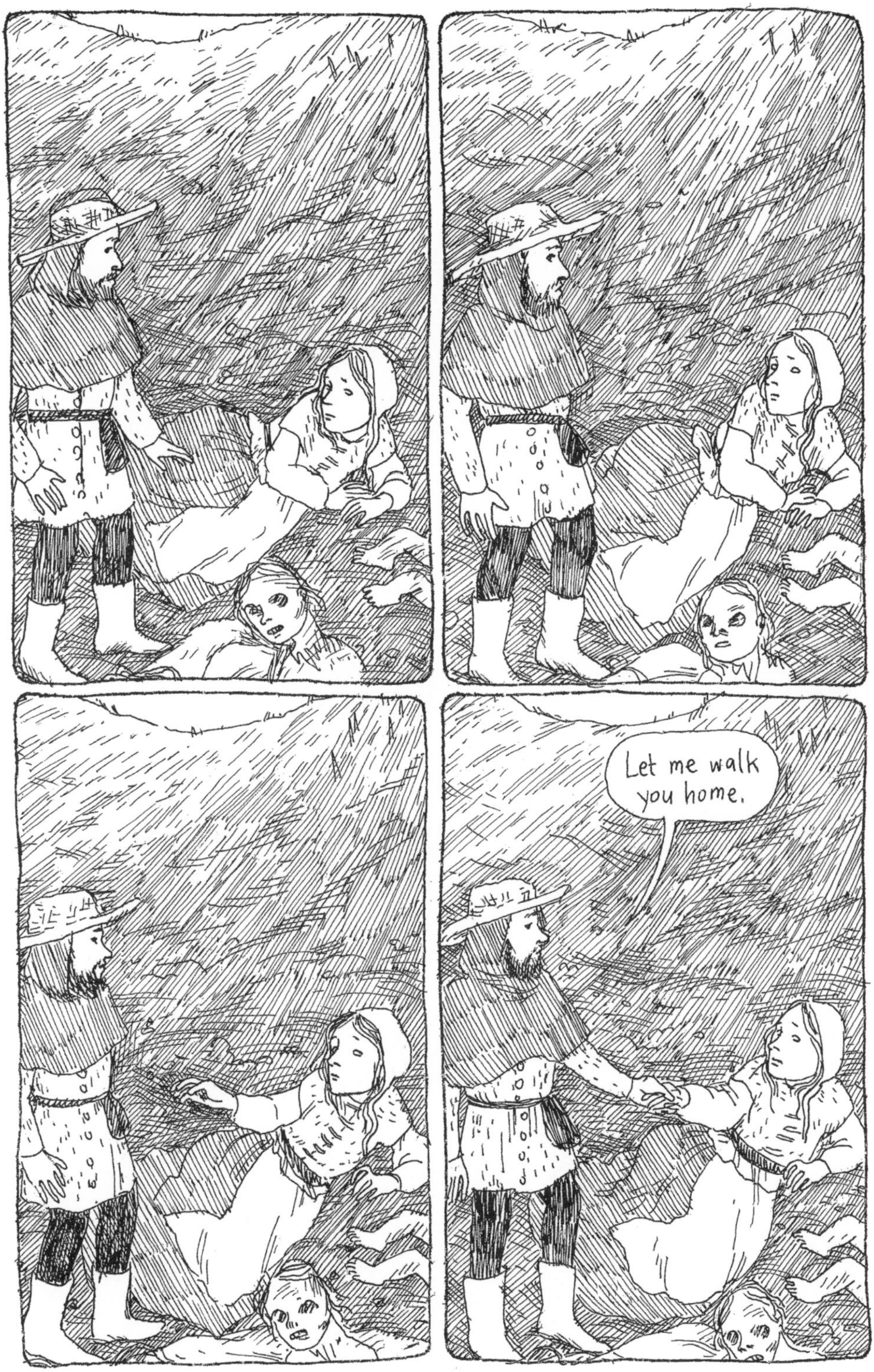
Let me walk you home.

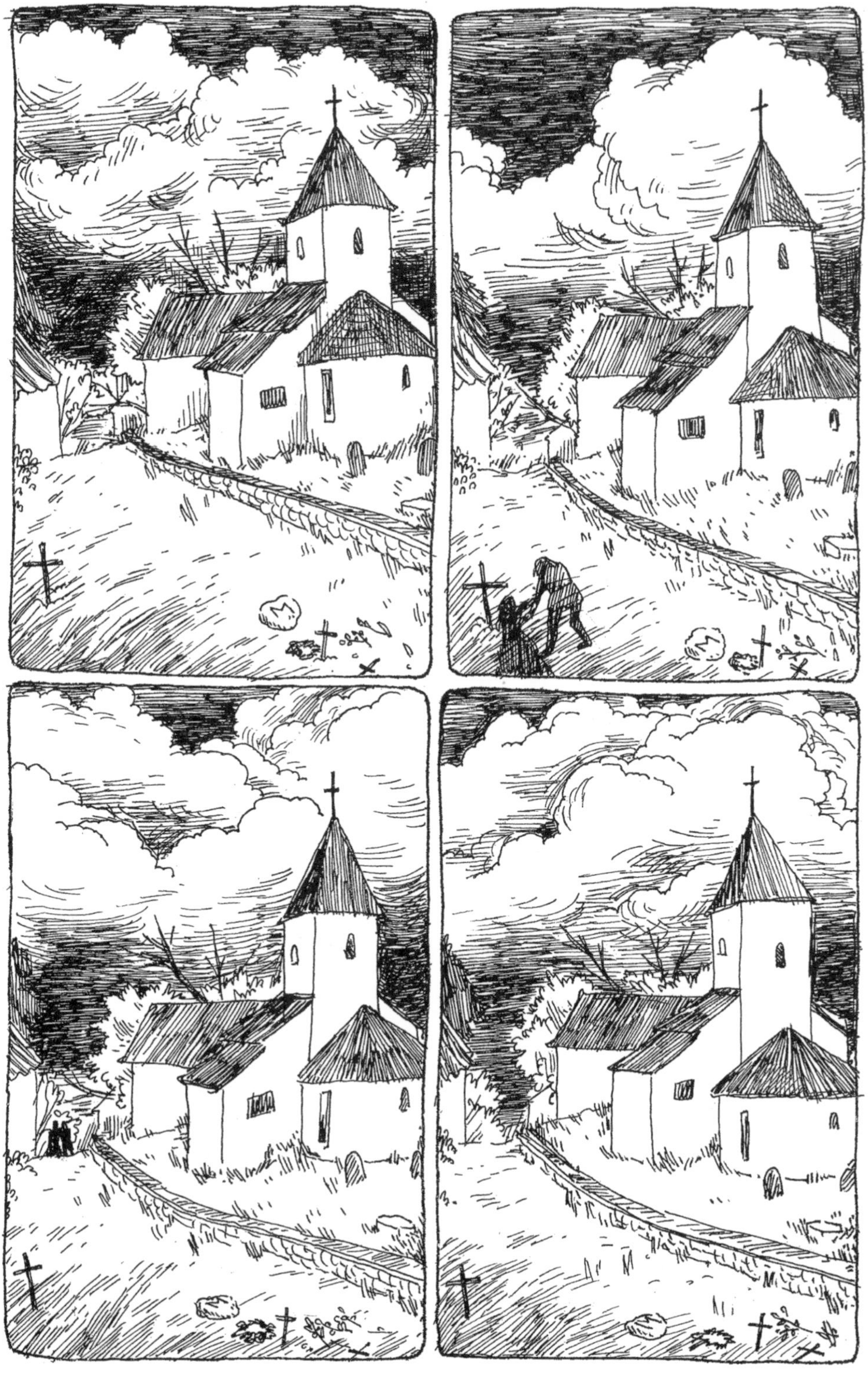

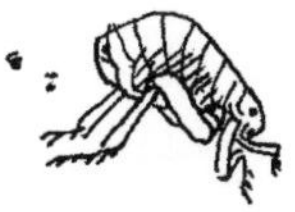

Julia Gfrörer was born in 1982 in Concord, NH, and currently lives in Floral Park, NY. Her first graphic novel, *Black Is The Color,* was published by Fantagraphics Books in 2013, and her work has also appeared in *Kramers Ergot* and *Best American Comics.*

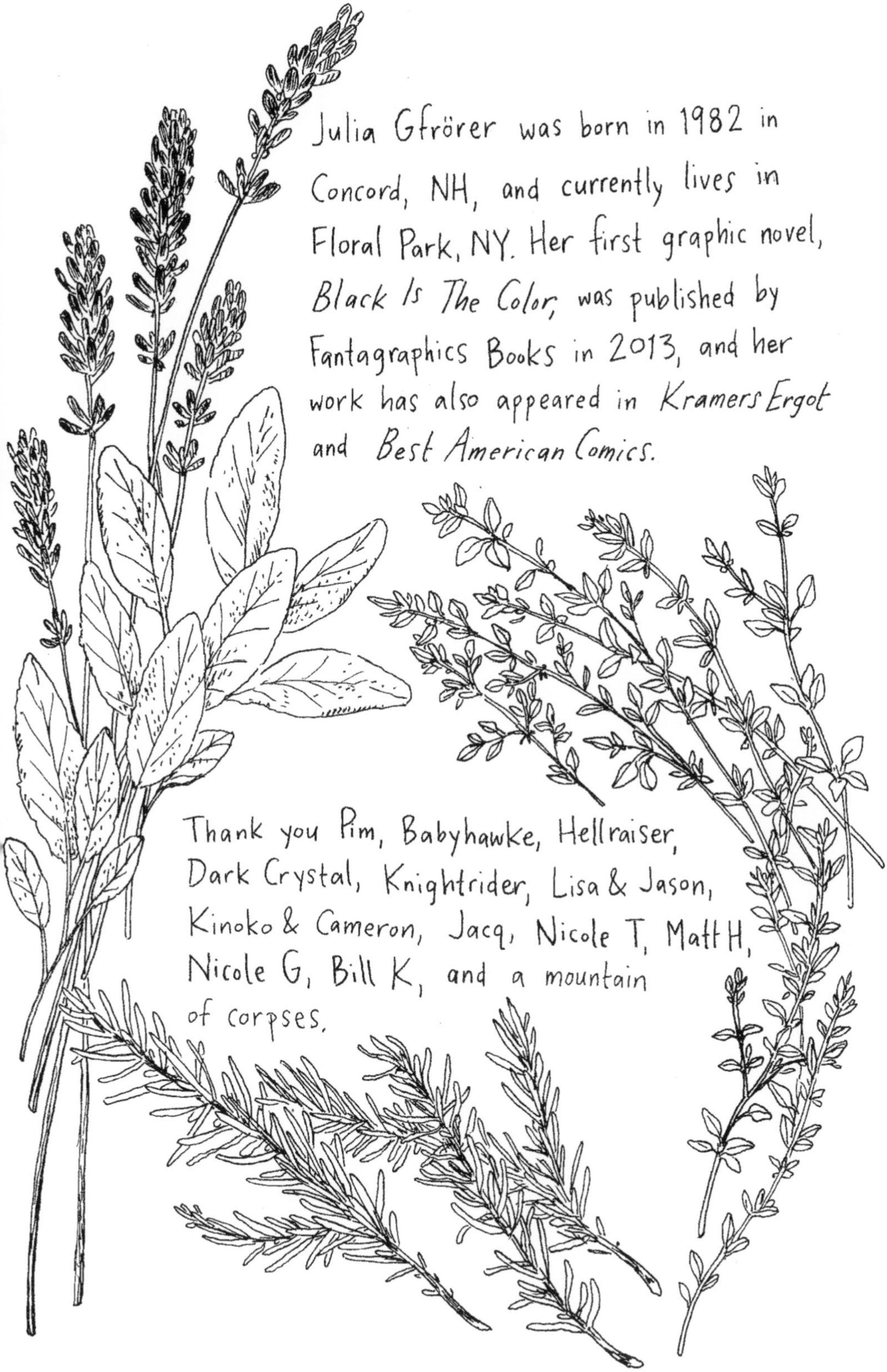

Thank you Pim, Babyhawke, Hellraiser, Dark Crystal, Knightrider, Lisa & Jason, Kinoko & Cameron, Jacq, Nicole T, Matt H, Nicole G, Bill K, and a mountain of corpses.

FANTAGRAPHICS BOOKS, INC.

Seattle, Washington, USA

Editor and Associate Publisher: Eric Reynolds
Book Design: Julia Gfrörer
Production: Paul Baresh
Publisher: Gary Groth

First printing: October 2016
Printed in Hong Kong

ISBN 978-1-60699-971-4

AUG 2 4 2017